"I'll stay with you for a week, Gideon, but I'm not promising any more than friendship," Serena said.

"Hush, don't spoil it." He lifted her hand to his lips and kissed her palm lingeringly. "Let me be happy."

"All right." Her voice was breathless, and the night was suddenly crackling with sensual electricity that made her heart start to pound wildly.

His clasp tightened around her wrist, and she knew he had felt her betraying leap of response. "For me?" he murmured. "Let's see what else I can . . ." His tongue gently stroked her palm, his thumb on her wrist monitoring her reaction. "You like that?"

She felt as if she'd been jolted by lightning. The slightest of intimacies, and she was trembling. "Let me go, Gideon."

"In a minute." He moved his lips to the delicate blue veins of her wrist. "I can feel your heartbeat going crazy. You're easy to arouse, love." He nipped her skin with his teeth and she felt a burst of heat flood her. "We're going to be so good together . . ."

WHAT ARE *LOVESWEPT* ROMANCES?

They are stories of true romance and touching emotion. We believe those two very important ingredients are constants in our highly sensual and very believable stories in the *LOVESWEPT* line. Our goal is to give you, the reader, stories of consistently high quality that may sometimes make you laugh, sometimes make you cry, but are always fresh and creative and contain many delightful surprises within their pages.

Most romance fans read an enormous number of books. Those they truly love, they keep. Others may be traded with friends and soon forgotten. We hope that each *LOVESWEPT* romance will be a treasure—a "keeper." We will always try to publish

*LOVE STORIES YOU'LL NEVER FORGET
BY AUTHORS YOU'LL ALWAYS REMEMBER*

The Editors

LOVESWEPT® • 191

Iris Johansen

Across the River of Yesterday

BANTAM BOOKS
TORONTO • NEW YORK • LONDON • SYDNEY • AUCKLAND

ACROSS THE RIVER OF YESTERDAY
A Bantam Book / May 1987

*For Karen Nevois, my friend,
who understands about
yesterdays . . . and tomorrows*

Mariba, Castellano

The girl's violet eyes were blank and dazed. She seemed scarcely aware of the trio of human carnivores who had backed her against the wall.

Gideon Brandt had seen that expression of dumb, uncomprehending torment once before, and he wanted to look away before the memories of the day in Na Peng came back to him. Hell, he was probably mistaken. It was smoky as the devil, the lighting in the bar was dim, and the girl was on the far side of the room. If she appeared dazed, it was probably because she was on something. Dope was cheap here in Mariba and sometimes it seemed to him that half the population of Castellano was stoned. The clinging white satin gown the girl wore plunged practically to her navel and she was here in Concepción's place. Those two facts should have made it obvious to him that she was one of Concepción's girls and here to serve the exact sexual purpose of the men surrounding her.

"Pretty little thing," Ross commented as he picked up his glass from the bar. His gaze appraised the girl critically. "Younger than Concepción usually hires them. Are you thinking about taking a trip upstairs later?"

Gideon scowled. "For Pete's sake, she can't be a day over sixteen. I don't go to bed with teenagers." He forced himself to look away from the girl across the room, and down at the bourbon in his glass. "And we're not here to try out Concepción's new merchandise. Where the hell is Ramón? You said he'd arrive before midnight."

"He'll be here. He was very interested in your proposition." Ross's gaze was still on the girl across the room. "Those three jaspers don't seem to have your reluctance to indulge in young meat. Their hands are all over her. Hell, they may not make it upstairs before—" He broke off and gave a low whistle. "Well, I'll be damned. She's barefoot."

"What?" Gideon's gaze swung back to the girl, who was backed against the far wall. She *was* barefoot. One naked foot peeped out from beneath the hem of the satin gown and for some reason that nudity made her appear even more vulnerable and childlike. As he watched, one of the men reached out and slowly covered the girl's right breast with his large hand and squeezed it.

She didn't flinch. She didn't appear to even feel it. Why was he so damn worried about a hooker who'd probably been turning tricks since she was an adolescent? She clearly didn't mind being fondled by anything in pants, so why should it bother him? He tossed down the rest of the bourbon in one swallow. It felt hot and good going down, but it didn't banish the uneasiness he was beginning to feel.

Ross studied Gideon, shrewdly assessing his mood. "You're edgy," he said at last. "I told you, nothing will go wrong with the deal. Ramón has been looking for a man like you for a long time. Why should you be worried? You'll soon be on easy street."

Gideon's lips twisted. "There is no easy street on Castellano. Even after you've got it all, you have to fight like hell to keep it."

He knew very well that this island in the Caribbean was one of the most lawless spots in the Southern Hemisphere, its government rivaling its inhabitants in corruption. The lawlessness of this place suited Gideon's purpose at the moment, but he had no illusions about longevity in Mariba. He intended to make his fortune and get out before someone could corner him in a back alley and slit his throat.

Ross gave another whistle. "Now, isn't that pretty?" He lifted his glass to his lips, not taking his gaze off the girl across the room. "I might just take a trip upstairs myself and leave you to talk to Ramón on your own."

Reluctantly, Gideon looked again at the girl's slender foot, then at the satin-clad slightness of her body. He inhaled sharply. One of the men had pushed down the strap of her white gown and her left breast was fully revealed: Velvet white, pink crested, surprisingly voluptuous.

He felt an unmistakable tightening in his groin

and the muscles of his stomach knotted in a response that was half anger and half lust. Dammit, before long they'd have her stripped naked for every man in the bar to gawk at. Why the hell didn't she choose one of those bastards and take him upstairs? Didn't she realize she was inviting a gang bang? He muttered a curse beneath his breath as his gaze lifted to her face.

She *didn't* realize it. He doubted if she even knew what was happening to her. It was Na Peng all over. Only this time he couldn't stand by and let it happen. He had been helpless then, but, by God, he wasn't helpless now.

He set his glass down on the bar. "Tell Ramón we'll have to postpone our little chat. I'll send word when I'm available for another meeting." He turned away from the bar.

"Where are you going?" Ross was staring at him, dumbfounded.

"The girl," Gideon said simply. "I'm going to get the girl."

"Right now? Can't it wait, for heaven's sake? She seems a little busy at the moment."

Gideon shook his head. "I'm going to get the girl," he repeated. "I don't think she knows what the hell is happening to her." He started across the room, his tall, lithe body suddenly radiating a near-explosive tension as he cut an unswerving path through the crowded tables toward the girl pinned against the wall in the back of the room.

Ross hesitated, his gaze on Gideon's broad shoulders. He had an impulse to hurry after him and try to persuade him to forget about the girl. Ramón was important to them both. What a helluva time for Gideon's protective instincts to surface. He quickly dismissed the impulse. Gideon might be swayed by arguments if it were a simple matter of his being hot for a choice little hooker, but not if he thought there was a possibility the girl was a victim. Ross was far too familiar with Gideon's large collection of lame ducks ever to make that mistake. Hell, he was part of that menagerie himself. He sighed morosely. So much for easy street.

He set his glass down and straightened away from the bar. Three against one. Saint George might need some help slaying his dragons. He threw a few bills down on the bar and sauntered slowly after Gideon.

"Get the hell out of here!"

Gideon dumped the girl in the backseat of the jeep and jumped in beside her.

Tables and chairs were crashing and splintering in the bar behind them while Concepción roared Spanish obscenities above the curses of the brawling patrons of her establishment. Gideon grinned with enjoyment and admiration. Concepción had a magnificent vocabulary.

Ross jumped into the driver's seat, jammed his foot on the gas, and the jeep lurched away from the curb. He cast a glance over his shoulder just as the door of the bar was thrown open, and Concepción, herself, appeared on the sidewalk. Her curses reached a new high in inventiveness as she shook her fist at them. Ross grimaced. "She's furious at us. You do realize what a sacrifice I made in helping you pluck your little pullet from Concepción's barnyard? She runs the best whorehouse on the island and she's not about to let either of us back in there after that brawl you started."

"It was the quickest way to get rid of those leeches who were fastened on the girl." Gideon shrugged. "A few indiscriminate punches and the whole place exploded." He leaned back in the seat and stretched his long legs as far as he could within the confines of the jeep. "And Concepción will welcome you back as soon as she gets over her little tantrum. You're one of her best customers whenever you come to Mariba."

"May I ask where we're going?" Ross asked dryly. "Now that you've got the girl, what are you going to do with her?"

"That's a good question." Gideon turned to the girl beside him. She hadn't said a word since he had appeared at her side, and had allowed herself to be picked up and handled as if she were a doll. Her breast was still naked and he experienced again the hot surge to his loins that signaled instant arousal. He carefully pulled the thin strap up and over her shoulder, then adjusted the satin over her breast. Close now, he could see she wasn't only pretty, she was truly lovely. Her long dark hair was midnight silk against her pale, perfect complexion, and those wonderful violet eyes lent startling beauty to her regular features. How the hell had Concepción gotten her hands on prime quality like this? The only thing lacking to complete her beauty was animation.

"What about it?" Gideon asked quietly. "Do you live in Mariba? Is there someplace we can take you where you'll be safe?"

She didn't answer. Gideon hadn't thought she would. It was obvious that an emotional shock of some sort had frozen the words inside her. What kind of shock? Rape was a definite possibility, but, if it had been rape, wouldn't she have responded when those apes in the bar were pawing her? Unless she had been given something. . . .

His hands reached out and grasped her shoulders. They felt silken-slender and infinitely delicate beneath his palms. He shook her slightly. "Look, are you on something? Were you given anything? Powders or pills or an injection of some kind?"

She didn't answer. Her gaze met his own with the same blind torment that had first caught his attention across the crowded barroom.

He slowly released her. "It's all right," he said softly. "You're safe now. I won't let anyone hurt you. Do you understand?"

She didn't answer.

"Okay." His voice was as gentle as his palm cupping her cheek. "Talk to me when you feel like it. I'll be here. Are you cold?" The wind was blowing her hair behind her in a gleaming ebony stream as the jeep negotiated the deserted streets. "It's cooling down. I think we're going to have a storm. Come here." He drew her closer, tucking her slight weight in the curve of his arm. "You're not exactly dressed for a midnight drive. Where did you leave your shoes?"

She remained silent, but he thought he could detect the slightest relaxation of the frozen stiffness that was enveloping her muscles.

"Not yet? Don't worry about it. There's no hurry."

His hand slowly stroked her temple and his voice was low. "You know, when something bad happens to me, I try to close it out at first and put it behind me. That doesn't mean one has to close out the present too. I have some friends among the Hopi Indians and they taught me something very interesting: They have no past or future tenses in their language. Only the present. It must save a lot of worrying." He tucked a silken strand of her hair behind her ear. "If you come back to me, I promise there won't be anything to frighten you. All you have to do is live minute by minute and not look back. Then, after a little while, you'll find that your wound has crusted over, and it won't hurt you nearly so much to think about it."

There was a tiny movement, almost a nestling against his shoulder.

He fought the urge to tighten his clasp around her shoulders. He continued to stroke the silky hair at her temple. "My name is Gideon Brandt and that's Ross Anders up front. What's your name?" It suddenly occurred to him that she might not understand English. She didn't look Spanish, but the majority of the population of Castellano were of Latin descent. "*¿Cómo se llama?*"

She drew a quivering breath and for a moment he thought she was going to speak. Then she was still, her long, dark lashes lowering to shadow the exquisite violet of her eyes.

"Well, if you don't understand English or Spanish, we may be out of luck. I'm just a good old Texas boy and those are the only lingoes I know."

"Are we going to drive around town all night?" Ross asked.

"No, I guess we'd better go home."

"Right." Ross turned left at the next corner.

"We're going to take you to my place," Gideon said into the girl's ear. "It's right on the edge of town. I won it in a poker game a few weeks ago, and it's a little run-down, but I think it's kind of pretty. I've been batting around the world since I was a kid and it's . . . it's nice to have a place that belongs to me. I have to warn you, the house is almost empty. The furniture wasn't thrown into the pot and I only made a deal with García to leave the bedroom and kitchen stuff. That was as far as he'd go. He even took the chandelier in the foyer. It's a two-story hacienda with a red-tiled roof and a patio with a fountain. The fountain doesn't work, and the patio has weeds growing between the tiles, but I'll get around to having it fixed up eventually. I've been too busy to bother. . . ." His voice droned on. He was paying little attention to what he said, merely trying to keep the patter bland and unthreatening. When your world had been blown to smithereens, it was always the ordinary that helped to balance the picture. He had found that out a long time ago.

The lights of the jeep suddenly illuminated two beautiful wrought-iron gates. They were standing open and one was hanging drunkenly from a broken bracket.

"I haven't had a chance to fix that either." Gideon made a face as the jeep turned into the pebbled circular road forming the driveway through tangled, overgrown foliage. "I wasn't expecting visitors quite so soon."

The silence was suddenly broken by loud barking interspersed with joyous whines. "Don't be afraid. That's only Frank, my dog. I think he's half Lab and half German shepherd, but only the stork knows for sure."

The jeep rounded a curve and a large white stucco house came into view. Ross drew to a halt at the front doors and turned off the ignition. The carved double doors were set in a deep alcove and illuminated by a single ornate brass lantern set in the distempered white wall.

Gideon jumped from his seat and lifted the girl carefully from the jeep to the patio. "Easy does it." He released her and stepped back to look at her in the glow of the lantern. Dear heaven, she was beautiful, and so heartbreakingly young and vulnerable that he felt guilty as hell about the sexual response her beauty aroused in him. "We'll just get you inside and find you a bed and some clean sheets and you'll—" He was forced to stop in midsentence as a large gray-and-tan fury of affection hurled itself between them, almost knocking the breath from Gideon's lungs. "Down, Frank." He rubbed the dog's ears and then pushed him away. The dog dropped to the ground, but still continued the whimpering cries of ecstatic welcome. "I've been meaning to teach him not to jump on people, but I haven't gotten around to that either. I've only had him for a few weeks. Maybe I'll try—"

"Why does he have only three legs?" The girl's voice was soft, hesitant.

Gideon's heart jerked and he drew a deep breath. Her gaze was on the dog, and as he watched she slowly reached out her hand to touch Frank's long muzzle. "I don't know." He spoke with deliberate casualness. "He was missing his right hind leg when I picked him up. Frank must have had a pretty rough life, judging by the battle scars I found when I was defleaing him."

"Some kids had tied him to the rear bumper of a truck and he was being dragged through the streets when Gideon first saw him," Ross said as he came around the front of the jeep to stand beside them.

"How cruel." An expression of disgust darkened her face. "How could anyone do something like that?" She dropped to her knees beside the large dog, her hand lovingly stroking his neck. "The poor thing."

"You like dogs?" Gideon asked.

"I love dogs. I've never been permitted to have a pet, but I've always wanted one."

Thank heaven for small favors, Gideon thought fervently. If sympathy and affection hadn't broken through her icy shock, it might have taken days before she reached this point. She was poised on a very precarious ledge, but at least she was back among the living. He would have to be cautious to make certain she didn't slip back. "Well, I'm sure Frank is glad to make your acquaintance . . ." He trailed off inquiringly.

"Serena," she supplied absently. "He looks hungry. Have you fed him today?"

Frank always looked hungry and was a con artist of the highest caliber, as Gideon well knew. "Maybe he could use a midnight snack." Gideon reached out his hand and pulled her to her feet. "Let's go scout around the kitchen and see what we can find for him, Serena."

"Okay." Her hand curled around his as trustingly as that of a small child.

"Ross, why don't you make up the bed in the guest room and see if you can find something for Serena to sleep in."

Ross nodded and turned to open the front door. "Right, it may come down to draping her in a sheet, but I'll find something."

Gideon smiled at Serena as he followed Ross into the house and flipped on the light in the foyer. "I believe we can avoid using the sheet, but I'm afraid you'll have to make do with one of my shirts. I don't think we can find a nightgown for you."

She frowned. "But why would I need a nightgown?" She touched the sleek satin of her bodice. "I'm wearing a nightgown." Then emotion flared behind the vagueness of her eyes, raw and hurting emotion that threatened to burn away the comforting veil of forgetfulness.

Gideon silently cursed his lack of luck in making the seemingly innocent remark. He said quickly, "I just thought you might want to change after you shower. Are you hungry? Maybe it would be a good idea if we found something for you to eat too." He took her elbow and gently propelled her down the corridor in the direction of the kitchen. The pain was fading from her expression and she was casually petting Frank's head as he trailed beside her down the hallway. "I'm not much of a gourmet cook, but I can whip up an omelet. Do you cook?"

She shook her head. "The sisters at the convent were always more interested in feeding our souls than our bodies." Her lips curved in a tiny smile. "Sister Maria said we thought far too much about the worldly pleasures."

A convent! "I wouldn't call eating a particularly worldly pleasure."

"You aren't Sister Maria."

"For which I'm profoundly grateful. I'm far too irreverent to fit into a religious community."

"I wasn't very comfortable there either." Her smile widened to breathtaking beauty. "I was always getting into trouble. I always laughed too much. In chapel and vespers and at—"

"Good." His hand tightened on her elbow. "I like a woman who laughs. The world doesn't have enough laughter to go around." He pushed opened the door to the kitchen and flicked on the ceiling light. "Now suppose you and Frank go sit over there at the table and watch me prepare the most splendiferous omelet you've ever tasted."

She smiled again and he felt his breath stop in his throat. What was going on here? One minute he felt only aching sympathy and the next he was ready to pull the girl into the nearest bedroom. She was the walking wounded, for heaven's sake. He turned away and opened a cabinet above the stove. "And you can tell me more about Sister Maria's definition of sin."

Serena finished the last bite of omelet and set her fork down on her plate. She had been very hungry, she realized with dull surprise. She tried to remember the last time she had eaten. It had been this morning at dawn. She had shared warm croissants and strong black coffee with— She shied away from the memory with a sense of panic. The Hopi Indians. No past and no future. Only now. Now was safe and free from pain. Gideon had told her this was true, and in a shifting world of lies, his words were the only honest, solid anchor to which she could cling.

"Maybe I'm not such a bad cook after all. You managed to clean up your plate anyway." He pushed back his chair and stood up. "I'll get you something to drink. I should probably give milk to someone as young as you, but I hate the stuff and never keep it in the house. How about some orange juice?" He crossed the room to the refrigerator on the far side of the kitchen. "It's the only nonalcoholic beverage I have."

"That will be fine." She watched the slide of muscles beneath his khaki shirt as he opened the refrigerator door. He was tall, over six feet, and every inch was lean and powerful. She suddenly had a hazy recollection of how those muscles had exploded into lethal, totally devastating force tonight in the bar. She couldn't seem to connect the memory with the man who had held her with almost feminine tenderness in the jeep, or the master Frank was gazing up at with such hopeful adoration. Surely no one could look less threatening. He was dressed in faded jeans that hung low on his lean hips and a short-sleeved khaki shirt, unbuttoned at the collar to reveal the strong line of his tan throat. He was wearing brown cowboy boots, scuffed and weathered by the elements. Weathered was the word that described more about him than his boots. He looked totally experienced, as if he had gone through all the storms and droughts life could offer and had emerged not broken, only seasoned and tougher.

His skin was tanned by sun and wind to a deep bronze and laugh lines radiated from the corners of his brown eyes. His hair might have been a dark brown at one time but now it was sun-streaked, tawny, slightly tousled with . . . a cowlick. She smiled when she noticed that unruly lock of hair. No, she must have been mistaken about the lethal side of Gideon Brandt she thought she'd glimpsed in the bar. Who could be afraid of a man with a cowlick? "I'm not really that young. I'm seventeen."

"So old? I've got ten years on you." He poured the juice into a tall glass and looked up to smile at her. Dimples. Deep slashing dimples indented his lean cheeks. The shape of his face was almost square, his features more rugged than handsome and his smile the warmest she had ever seen. She suddenly felt as if she had been enfolded in a magical fleecy blanket, gossamer light yet capable of generating sunlight and tenderness and . . . His gaze held her own as he walked toward her with lithe, vital grace. "You look younger."

"Do I?" She didn't feel young. She felt a million years old and suddenly so weary she had to keep her spine very straight to keep from falling off the chair.

He nodded and there was a flicker of under-standing in his face, almost as if he had read her thoughts. "You'll feel young again, you know," he said gently. "Maybe you'll never be a child again, that's probably gone forever, but youth remains.

Sometimes we have to work to keep it alive in us, but it's important we never lose a sense of youth and joy." He grinned and the creases deepened around his eyes and in the long dimples on each side of his mouth. "Personally, I intend to still be a kid when I am a hundred and two."

"I think you'll make it," she said softly.

"I'm sure I will." He set the glass of orange juice down in front of her. "And so will you. Now, drink. You'll need your vitamins if you want to survive and stay healthy." His gaze met hers. "And you do want to survive. Life can be damn good, and you can solve any problem if you just face up to it." He reached down and patted the dog's head. "Ask Frank here. He's a prime example."

"He had help."

"So will you, if you'll accept it." Gideon carefully kept his gaze on the dog's mottled fur. "And he probably didn't have any help when he lost that leg. He survived it all by himself and still didn't lose the capacity to care. Toughen up, but keep the loving. It's important, Serena." He straightened. "Now I'd better stop this preaching and feed this particular survivor. He's been giving me a guilt trip ever since I started cooking your omelet."

"I noticed." Serena took a drink of the orange juice. "I also noticed you gave him half of that pound of bacon you sprinkled on my omelette."

He made a face. "So I'm a sucker."

"That's what I've been telling you for two years." Ross stood in the doorway. He strolled forward, a grin lighting his plain features. "Do you know why I had to put Frank's bowl and food out on the patio, Serena? The first two days after we brought him home, he gained five pounds and we each lost three."

Serena laughed. In spite of Ross's caustic tone, it was clear the bond of affection between the two men was very strong. Strange. They appeared to be complete opposites, both in physique and personality. Ross was a few inches under six feet and built with blocky muscularity and deep-chested strength. He was closer to forty than thirty, and his dark hair was flecked with silver. The blue eyes looking into her own were shrewd, and she had an idea the affectionate smile softening his face as he regarded Gideon could turn cynical in the flicker of a second.

Ross turned to her. "Your chamber awaits. It's the first guest room at the top of the stairs."

"She has to finish her orange juice first," Gideon said. "Stay with her while I take Frank out and feed him. Did you light the hot water heater?"

Ross nodded and explained to Serena. "The gas heater is an antique and the pilot light keeps going out on us." His lips twisted. "Another thing we're going to get fixed." He waved his hand. "Go on and feed the bottomless pit. I'll watch over your other . . . over Serena."

Stray. He had been about to call her a stray, Serena thought. The realization brought no resentment. Rather it filled her with a comfortable sense of security to be referred to as belonging in any way to Gideon Brandt. He obviously showered those he took under his wing with warmth and love and she desperately needed that security to help fight off the darkness surrounding her.

She watched Gideon leave the kitchen, the big

dog skittering unevenly at his heels. "He's so kind," she said huskily. "Have you known him long?"

"A few years. We met in Tucson and took to each other right away. We've been together ever since." He sat down and nodded to the glass in her hand. "You'd better finish that. He won't let you go to sleep until you drink it down."

She laughed uncertainly. "You have to be joking. Gideon wouldn't force me to drink something I didn't want."

"He won't ever force you, but you'll find yourself doing what he wants anyway." He shrugged. "It's easier just to do what he tells you in the beginning."

She took another swallow of orange juice. "I think you're mistaken. He's too gentle to—"

"I didn't say he wasn't gentle," Ross interrupted briskly. "He's one hell of a human being and the best friend I've ever had. I'm just saying there's another aspect to his character that's equally strong."

She frowned. "And what is that?"

"When he makes up his mind, he's completely relentless. He never stops. Not ever. He might feel compassion, but it doesn't sway him. He never quits until he has what he wants."

She shook her head in disbelief.

"Yes," Ross said flatly. "It's something you should know, because I don't think Gideon has quite made up his mind about you yet. He's chewing it over and trying to come to a conclusion. Once he does, there's no way out. Gideon will be as much a prisoner of his determination as you, and probably more vulnerable. Something has knocked you for a loop and I'm sorry, but my first loyalty is to Gideon."

"You act as if you think I'm going to try to hurt him," she whispered. "How could I . . . I would never do anything to hurt anyone." There was too much pain in the world and not enough laughter. Gideon had said something like that, she remembered vaguely. He had said a great many things tonight. All with a touch as light as a summer breeze, with an underlying salve that had healed before she had even realized any balm had been applied.

"I just thought I'd drop in a savvy word or two. No offense?" Ross smiled. "Gideon would have a fit if he thought I'd upset you. Don't worry, he'll see to it that you're well taken care of."

She smiled back at him. "Like his other 'strays'?"

He grimaced. "You caught that? I was hoping I'd covered myself in time. I didn't mean to hurt your feelings."

"You didn't." She took another sip of orange juice. "How many strays does Gideon have here?"

"On the premises? Just one cat and a blind parrot. He usually tries to find homes for them before they become too attached to him. He moves around a lot and he doesn't think it's fair to leave them alone." He stood up. "Now, drink the rest of that down and I'll take you to your room."

The tall glass was still a quarter full. She deliberately pushed the glass away. "I've had enough." She scooted back her chair and rose to her feet. "I'm ready to go."

"Are you?" A curious smile touched his lips as his gaze rested on the glass. "Some people just have to learn for themselves." He turned away. "I found a clean shirt of Gideon's for you to wear tonight and I put a pair of my shorts and a T-shirt on the chair in your room for you to wear tomorrow. They'll be a little big, but I'm smaller than Gideon."

"Thank you. I'm sorry to be so much trouble."

"No trouble. These little adventures are what make living with Gideon interesting."

A glass of orange juice was on the white rattan nightstand beside the double bed when she came into the bedroom after her shower thirty minutes later. The glass was exactly one quarter full.

Gideon was lounging in the cane-backed chair by the window, one leg over the arm, a booted foot swinging lazily. "Hi, you look better in that shirt than I do. It kinda reminds me of those ads on TV where they have all those luscious ladies wearing their men's dress shirts."

"Does it? I've never seen them. They didn't have a television set at the convent." She touched the soft blue cotton of the shirt that came almost to her knees. "Thank you for lending it to me. It's very comfortable."

"We aim to please." He swung his foot to the floor and stood up. He exuded so much power and vitality that Serena suddenly felt very small and helpless.

"I'm glad you didn't wash your hair. It must take a long time to dry and I was worried you'd go to bed with it wet." He crossed the room and drew back the top sheet. "In you go. I'll tuck you in and turn out the light."

She found herself obediently sliding into bed. He drew the sheet up around her shoulders and sat down beside her. "I've left the windows open. The screens will keep out the critters and it will be cooler for you. If it starts to rain, you'd better get up and close it." His gaze was gravely holding her own while his hand stroked the hair back from her temple. "You've done just fine so far, but I thought I'd better warn you that sometimes it comes back to you right before you go to sleep. It sort of waits like a bushwhacker until all your defenses are down and then it ambushes you." He smiled. "You just fool it and start thinking of something else. Frank or Ross or me . . . anything. Okay?"

"Okay," she whispered.

"And, if you get scared or want company, I'm just across the hall. I'll leave my door open to hear if you call out."

"Thank you." His hand on her temple held mesmerizing gentleness and his expression was . . . beautiful. "Gideon, I. . . ." She trailed off as she felt the tears burn behind her lids. "Just thank you. For everything."

"For nothing." His grin lit up his rough features with warmth. "All I did was cook you an omelet and lend you my shirt." He touched the tip of her nose with his index finger. "Go to sleep now and remember my very wise Hopi friends." He leaned forward and brushed her forehead with his lips as if she were a small child, *his* child. "Sleep tight."

"You too."

"I always sleep well." He rose and looked down

at her. "You just have to remember to watch out for those ambushes."

"You have them, too?"

"We all have them." He smiled again. "You're not alone, Serena." His gaze suddenly fell on the glass on the nightstand. "You forgot to drink your orange juice, so I emptied it out and brought you some fresh. Just what you need for a nightcap." He sat down again, picked up the glass and gathered her up into the curve of his arm. "Bottoms up."

"No, I don't—"

"Shh." His voice was velvet soft and coaxing. "You need it." He smiled that smile that enfolded her in sunlight and caring. "Come on, there's just a little in the glass and I want to feel I've done my duty to appease the gods of nutrition. I didn't have any milk to give you. You wouldn't want to make me feel bad, would you?"

Who would ever want Gideon Brandt to know sadness or discomfort? He was everything that was caring and loving, and so dear she could feel her throat tighten with emotion as she looked up at him. What difference did it make if she didn't want the orange juice? It wouldn't hurt her. She opened her lips and finished off the juice in a few swallows. As he took the glass away, she wrinkled her nose at him. "Satisfied?"

He nodded as he set the empty glass on the nightstand and laid her back against the pillows. "For now. You've been a very sensible girl." He stood up and flicked off the lamp. She could see his shadow move across the room to the door.

"Now watch out for those bushwhackers and get to sleep." He paused at the door. She couldn't see his face but she didn't need to see it. It was all there in his quiet voice. "I'm here for you, Serena. Always."

A moment later, he was gone, leaving the door ajar.

He heard the swift patter of her feet on the tiles and knew she was coming to him.

He had been lying awake, thinking and listening to the thunder and the rain beating against the tile roof. He had always liked rain. There had been precious little of it in the desert country where he had grown up and, when it did come, it was like a blessing on the parched land.

"Gideon?" Serena's voice was shaky and uncertain. She was standing in the doorway.

"I'm awake. Bushwhackers?"

"I did what you told me and went to sleep, but the thunder woke me and—"

"Ambush," he finished for her. He sat up in bed. "Bad luck. I hoped you'd get a good night's sleep. Come here."

She hesitated. "I don't want to bother you. I only thought . . ." She stopped. "I don't know what I thought."

"You thought you'd come see your friend and together we'd blow those bushwhackers to kingdom come." He chuckled. "Now come over here and we'll get down to it."

She came slowly to him. "Shall I turn on the light?"

"Not unless you want to. Sometimes darkness is better. You might toss me that robe on the chair. I'm naked as a jaybird and I don't want to shock your convent sensibilities." He stood up and shrugged into the white terry cloth robe she handed him. "There. Now come to bed and snuggle." He drew back the sheet, pushed Serena down on the bed and then lay beside her, pulling her into his arms. She smelled clean and sweet and felt wonderfully right in his arms. As he tightened his clasp about her he realized she was trembling. He had thought she would be when he had heard her voice. She wouldn't have come to him if the pain of suppressing those memories hadn't been impossible to bear alone. He experienced a sudden aching regret as he realized what that meant. It was time.

He cradled her cheek against his shoulder, his palm cupping the back of her head. Thank heaven, she had come to him. She was very close to breaking, and she mustn't be alone when it happened. "Now, we're going to talk a little. Is that all right with you?"

"Yes." The assent was muffled against his shoulder.

"I think it's time we got to know each other. I was born on a little ranch in Texas and spent most of my childhood there. We lost the ranch when I was thirteen, and my parents died that same year. I was in an orphanage until I was sixteen and then wandered around the country, taking any job that came along." His fingers were soothingly rubbing her temple. "Then Vietnam and some more wandering. Recently I decided it would be better to be rich than to be poor, so I guess I'll have to settle down for a while. Ross will be very relieved. He has a taste for the good things of life. There. Now you know all about Gideon Brandt, Esquire." He looked down at her. "Have I talked you to sleep?"

"No."

"Are you an only child?"

"No, I have a younger brother. I don't see much of him. He attends school in England. My stepfather was awarded custody of—" She broke off and he felt her stiffen against him. "I don't want to talk about it."

"You don't have to talk about it, you don't have to talk about anything." His voice was very soft. "But it's time we shot those bushwhackers out of the saddle and there's only one way to do it, Serena."

"Gideon, I—"

"Shhh. You've got to invite them in and let them take their shot at you. You've got to remember. Then you'll be in control again."

She could feel the panic rising within her. "*No!*"

"Yes." His voice was totally certain and she suddenly remembered that Ross had called him relentless. "It's time to face it. Then it will be all over and you can start to heal. You're not alone. I'm here. I'm holding you. Now, *remember*, Serena."

She began to shake as if in the throes of malaria. "Gideon . . ."

"Don't talk about it, unless you want to, but admit to yourself that it happened. It *did* happen."

"No!" The word was uttered through clenched teeth. "Don't make me!"

"You were in your nightgown, and your feet were bare."

And she remembered.

The tears were suddenly raining down her cheeks and harsh sobs were wracking her body. "Ugly. Oh, God, so much ugliness. Gideon . . ."

"It's all right, baby." His voice was a low croon in her ear. "It's all over, it's gone now."

"It will never be gone. I'll always see . . ."

"No, you'll always remember, but after a while you won't see it anymore. There are so many beautiful things in the world, and I'll show them all to you. Whenever you start to remember, I'll pull another one out of the hat and then it will fade away again." His voice was a level above a whisper as his hand stroked her hair. "Do you believe me, Serena?"

"I don't know. I just don't . . ." The sobs were no longer tearing at her body, but she couldn't seem to stop the tears from flowing. "I can't *think*."

"Then I'll quit my jawing and let you rest." His lips touched the top of her head. "I'm not going to hassle you, baby. Relax now. You can think about what I said later. Right now, we'll talk about something else. What do you want to do?"

The sudden switch of subjects bewildered her. "Do?"

"You know, do you want to swim the English Channel or be a clown in a circus or be the first lady to go to Mars?"

"Oh." She wiped her wet cheeks with the back of her hand. "I've always wanted to be an artist. I love to paint. My mother took me to the Louvre once when I was a little girl and someday I'm . . ." She trailed off, floundering. She was actually thinking about the future, she realized with astonishment.

"See?" Gideon said softly. "There is a tomorrow. Now that you've faced the past, you can go on. One of these days you'll be as famous as Titian or Da Vinci or Rubinoff. Will you paint me a picture?"

Her arms tightened around him. "I'll paint you a mural," she said with passionate intensity. "I'll paint you your own Sistine Chapel, if you like."

He chuckled. "I appreciate the gesture, but a painting will do. A Serena original."

The tears had stopped. The wound was still throbbing, but it was already beginning to heal. "You'll have it," she whispered. She wanted to give him the moon, gift-wrapped. He had given her so much. "Anything you want."

He became very still. "Lord, I wish you hadn't said that. I'm trying to remember what a youngster you are." His hand resumed its gentle stroking. "Listen, before you came I was lying here thinking about you, about us. When I was over in the Far East I picked up a lot of kind of strange ideas and one of them is about destiny. I believe some things are meant to be. Some people are meant to be together." He paused. "I think *we're* meant to be together, Serena. I know it sounds crazy, but almost from the first I realized we were right for each other. Can't you feel it? We're meant to love each other, to pleasure each other and help each other to be everything we can be. Why else were we both in that bar tonight? I think it must have been because we've been heading for each other all our lives and the time has come for us to be together. Now you're going to belong to me and I'm going to belong to you."

Serena felt a wild surge of joy. To belong to Gideon would be to belong to gentleness, laughter and beauty. Then her spirits plummeted. It wasn't possible. Sin. She couldn't take any more than she already had from Gideon. "No, I can't . . ."

"Hush." He placed two fingers over her lips to silence her. "I know you're not ready to think about any of this yet, but I wanted you to know how I felt. I'm not going to push you. You've still got some growing up to do, and I have to make enough money to keep us comfortable. But after all that's taken care of, we'll be together. It's important we both know that's going to happen."

Serena felt her throat tighten painfully. In a way this pain was worse than what she had undergone before. "Gideon, there's no way."

"There's always a way. We'll just have to find it." His fingers moved from her lips to cover her eyes. "I'll start working on it in the morning. Go to sleep now."

He wouldn't listen. He was already assuming control with the loveable autocracy she was beginning to recognize as a primary element of his character.

He never stops. Not ever. Ross's word came back to her and she felt a wild surge of regret and despair. He would face that ugliness and try to conquer it, but she couldn't stand that to happen.

"You're worrying again."

She shook her head. "No, not really."

"Then what are you thinking about?"

"Your Hopi Indian friends." Now. Snatch joy and safety now, for it might be a long time before she felt this happy again. "Tell me how you came to know them. Tell me all the places you've been and the people you've met and . . . oh, everything."

"Bedtime stories?" He laughed softly. "Okay. I guess I can think of some that aren't X-rated. I've done most everything at one time or another, from riding the rodeo circuit to roughing it on an oil rig. I never finished high school so I had to stick to what I knew. Once when I was about your age I got a job on a freighter to the South Seas and . . ." His voice murmured on, spinning stories, sharing experiences, giving her glimpses into a life rich with color and the sheer joy of living.

He finally stopped and she could sense him looking down at her. She knew he thought she had fallen asleep. He carefully settled her closer against him and she felt again the gossamer touch of his lips against her forehead. She didn't move and kept her eyes firmly closed. Soon she felt his long, lean body relax and the sound of his breathing. He was asleep.

Serena's eyes opened and she stared unseeingly into the darkness.

The rain had stopped by the time the gray of predawn touched the horizon. Serena paused in the doorway to look back at Gideon still asleep in the big double bed. His tawny hair was rumpled on the pillow and he was sprawled like a weary little boy tucked into bed after a long day at play. She experienced a moment of maternal tenderness before she forced herself to turn and walk quickly across the hall. She hurriedly slipped on Ross's khaki shorts, but left on the blue shirt in which she had slept. It belonged to Gideon and surely it wouldn't hurt to keep a remembrance.

She had to try two doors along the corridor before she found Ross's room. She moved quietly across the shadowy room to stand beside his bed. "Ross?"

The figure beneath the sheets growled, mumbled and then raised himself on one elbow. "Serena?"

"I want you to take me back to the waterfront," Serena said quietly. "Now."

"The hell you do." He sat up and the sheet fell to his waist to reveal a brawny hair-roughened chest. "Gideon would cut my throat if I took you back to that bar."

She looked at him in surprise. "Why would I want to go back there? I wandered in there by mistake and . . ." She made an impatient gesture with her hand. "I just want you to take me to the waterfront and drop me off. I'd walk, but I don't have any shoes and I'm not sure of the way."

"Just drop you off." Ross's lips twisted. "Drop you on the streets of one of the wickedest cities in the Caribbean, barefoot and with no place to go."

"I have a place to go."

"Then wake up Gideon and tell him about it."

"I can't." She moistened her lower lip with her tongue. "You remember what you said about Gideon not having made up his mind about me yet?"

"Yes."

"Well, I think he's made it up now."

Ross's dark eyes narrowed on her face. "So?"

"It's impossible."

"Gideon doesn't understand the meaning of the word."

"Ross." She swallowed and then drew a deep breath, "I'm married."

He went still. Then he gave a long, low whistle. "Trouble."

She shook her head, blinking rapidly to keep back the tears. "Please, I don't want to hurt Gideon. I'm all right now. It will be perfectly safe to take me back."

"To your husband?"

She closed her eyes for a fraction of a moment and then opened them again. They held only sadness and determination. "To my husband."

He hesitated. "You're sure this is what you want?"

"I'm sure."

"Then I'll take you. Go on downstairs and wait in the jeep while I get dressed."

She turned away.

"You know this probably won't do you a damn bit of good. Gideon's not going to give up."

"He'll give up." Serena started for the door.

She heard a sharp bark of laughter behind her. "You don't know him at all if you think that." His voice was soft and slightly amused. "Tell me, Serena, did you ever drink the rest of the orange juice?"

She paused, her hand closing on the door knob. "That was different."

"Was it?" The amusement deepened. "I'll do what you ask, but don't think running away will do you any good if Gideon decides he wants to find you."

She drew a shaky breath and opened the door. "Please hurry. I want to be gone before Gideon wakes up." She closed the door behind her and walked quickly down the hall toward the curving staircase.

One

"Now, don't get excited." Dane's voice was soothing. "It's not as bad as it sounds."

Serena Spaulding counted to five. "What do you mean, it's not as bad as it sounds?" She pronounced every word distinctly into the telephone receiver. "How could it be worse? You tell me you've been flung into a Latin American jail on a drug charge, and that they're threatening to throw away the key and forget you ever existed. Sounds fairly serious to me."

"But it's all a mistake. You know I'm not into drugs. I think *they* even know it's a mistake, but they want to save face by putting on a big show of authority. All you have to do is come down and vouch for my character and they'll release me into your custody."

"Dane, they don't put people into jail and then release them so easily. I'd better call the American Consulate."

"No!" Dane's voice was suddenly sharp. "You know the first thing they'll do is call Mother and she'll call—" He broke off. "Look, it's very simple. I'll be off this island within a day, if you'll just come down and sign their damn papers. I tell you, they know they're in the wrong. I'm not even in a regular jail. They've put me up in a fancy hotel and they're wining and dining me as if I were a VIP. They even sent me a call girl last night. Does that sound like you're going to run into any trouble?"

"No." Serena wearily rubbed her temple. It sounded absolutely crazy, but what else could she expect from her brother? He had fallen into one brouhaha after another from the day he had discovered how amusing life could be if you didn't conform to any of the rules. And she had found it amusing, too, she admitted to herself. Involving herself in Dane's occasional adventures lent a badly needed touch of color to her life, to the regime of hard work and self-discipline she imposed upon herself. There was no question that Dane provided plenty of that color. However, he had never been thrown into prison before. She had a sudden memory of a horrifying film she had seen on television about a young man who had been arrested in Turkey on a drug charge. But this wasn't Turkey, she assured herself quickly, this was . . . Lord, she didn't even know where he was. "Dane, where the devil are you?"

There was a crackling on the line and then Dane's voice came clearly. "Just contact Colonel Pedro Mendino when you arrive. They have me quartered at the Hotel Cartagena."

"All right, I'll come right away, but where *are* you, dammit?"

"I told you. I'm in Mariba, Castellano. I have to hang up now. See you soon."

Mariba. Serena slowly replaced the receiver. The shock that had rippled through her was totally irrational. It wasn't as if she hadn't heard the name many times in the last ten years. Castellano was a hotbed of drug-running and smuggling and lately had been in the news constantly because of a revolutionary group challenging the military junta that governed the island.

She had simply grown accustomed to thinking of Mariba through a kind of dreamlike haze, which had nothing to do with her present existence. Now, abruptly, it was no longer far away. Her brother was imprisoned under wildly improbable circumstances, and she was going to return there after ten years.

She closed her eyes and drew a long quivering breath. Why was that night in Mariba suddenly so alive for her again? There had been months when she had forgotten about it entirely, and when she did remember, it was as if she were watching a film starring another woman entirely. The woman she was now bore no resemblance to the frightened girl who had clung to a stranger all through a long, stormy night. Ghosts. The girl she had been was a phantom, and so were Gideon Brandt and Ross Anders and the ramshackle ruin of a house on the outskirts of Mariba. None of it existed for her any longer. There was only the hardwon reality of the life she had created for herself. Was Gideon still there? The chances were very slim; he had been a wanderer and Castellano was not a place where anyone stayed for long. He probably was somewhere on the other side of the world, regarding the memory of their night together with the same remoteness she did. If he remembered her at all.

She turned briskly away from the phone. She'd have to close up the cottage and pack tonight. Tomorrow on the way to the airport she would stop at the bank and take out a sizeable amount of money and put it into traveler's checks. The situation in Mariba sounded weird in the extreme. Those papers Dane's jailers wanted her to sign very likely would have a high price tag, if everything she had heard about the government of Castellano were true.

"I think we're going in the wrong direction," Serena repeated, leaning forward to tap the taxi driver on the shoulder. "Perhaps you didn't understand me, it's the Cartagena Hotel and I'm sure we passed it five minutes ago. I saw a sign—"

"Si, the Hotel Cartagena." The driver smiled over his shoulder, his white teeth gleaming below his wide black mustache. "We are going in the right direction. You will see." The cab suddenly leaped forward as he pressed the accelerator. "I will get you there pretty damn quick."

"Not too quick," Serena said dryly as she leaned back in the seat. "I'd prefer to get there in one piece." Maybe there were two Hotel Cartagenas. It didn't seem likely in a town the size of Mariba, but the driver seemed very sure there was no mistake.

She opened her soft leather bag, took out a linen handkerchief and dabbed at her forehead. Heavens, it was hot. She would have to pick a taxi with no air conditioning. Not that she'd had much choice. There had only been two taxis available at the taxi stand at the airport, and she supposed she should be grateful to get transportation at all. Castellano's raffish reputation didn't foster it as a tourist spot, and she had seen larger private airports in the States.

Maybe she *had* been the one making the mistake. She had seen Mariba only at night and the town seemed totally unfamiliar to her in daylight, and there was no question she had been tense and on edge since the moment the small propeller plane had landed. It was idiotic to be so nervous, she assured herself. She would sign the papers, pay the bribe, and she and Dane would be off this island tomorrow.

"Right ahead," the driver said cheerfully. "I told you it would be pretty damn . . ." He trailed off as he stopped before a wrought-iron gate and blew the horn. The gates began to swing open slowly. "Electric. Pretty damn neat, huh?"

"Very neat." Serena's lips curved in amusement. Modern technology had evidently come even to Castellano. In this case, efficiency had not been allowed to interfere with the exquisite workmanship of the gates. They closed behind them with a quiet *swoosh* and the taxi started up the tree-lined drive.

The gardens of the hotel were really lovely. Beautifully manicured lawns unfolded before her like a bolt of emerald velvet, orderly beds of tropical flowers bloomed with vivid color, and Jasmine trees were bowed with fragrant white blossoms. If the hotel was as beautiful as its grounds, Dane must be very comfortable. . . .

She drew in her breath so sharply it made her dizzy. They had rounded the curve and a two-story house stood before them. Red tiled roof, gleaming white stucco walls, a fountain spraying sparkling water set in a patio. It was all crazily familiar. A dog should be barking, she thought half hysterically. It should be dark, not daylight and Frank should be running. . . .

"We are here." The driver drove up before the front door with a little flourish.

"This is no hotel." Her lips felt as if they didn't belong to her. "You've brought me to the wrong place."

The driver got out of the car and hurried around to open the door for her. "It is a little surprise. The Texan wants to see you."

"The Texan," she repeated numbly. "And just who is the Texan?"

"Gideon. Who else?" Ross Anders stepped out of the shadows of the front door alcove. "Hello, Serena. How are you?" His dark eyes went over her admiringly. "Besides being very beautiful, very elegant, and very sophisticated?"

"Fine." She moistened her lips with her tongue. "Just fine. How are you?" He looked very much the same as the last time she had seen him. There was a little more gray in his hair and he was wearing a steel-gray business suit that fit his blocky form with tailored elegance. She automatically identified it: Saville Row.

He smiled and stepped forward to help her out of the car. "Very well." He turned to the taxi driver. "Good job, Luis. Take her luggage out of the trunk and set them on the patio. I'll have one of the servants bring them in later."

Serena was suddenly jarred out of the stunned bewilderment into which she had been plunged when she'd seen the house. "*No*, I can't stay. I have to go to the hotel." She turned to the driver who was now at the trunk, busily extricating her suitcase. "Put it back in the trunk. I'm not staying."

The driver ignored her except for his beaming smile, which was beginning to annoy her exceedingly. He took the bag from the trunk and set it down.

"Did you hear me? I'm *not* staying."

"You are, you know," Ross said softly. "Luis isn't going to take you anywhere we don't want you to go. Gideon is in the library discussing business. Why don't you let me take you to your room to freshen up?"

"This is crazy." Serena could hear her voice tremble and tried to steady it. "Look, I have to go to my brother. He needs me."

He chuckled. "He needs absolutely nothing at the moment. He's being kept very well entertained."

"You know about Dane?" Serena asked incredulously.

Ross smiled. "He's a nice kid, a little wild, but he's got the right stuff. His coloring reminds me a little of you, Serena, but I understand he's only a half brother?"

"Yes," she said dazedly.

"He plays a mean game of poker." Ross's hand was on her elbow, propelling her gently toward the front door. "I nearly lost my shirt to him last night."

"They let you see him?"

"Oh yes, Gideon has me check on him every evening to make sure he's comfortable. Pedro Mendino can be . . . unpredictable."

Fear rained through her. "What do you mean unpredictable? Is Dane safe?"

Ross opened the door. "As in his mother's arms. Don't worry. Gideon won't let anything happen to Dane."

"Don't worry?" Serena whirled to face him, her violet eyes blazing. "What do you mean, don't worry? My brother has been imprisoned, I've been brought here and told I can't go anywhere without Gideon's permission and now you say this colonel who's holding Dane is 'unpredictable'! Why the hell shouldn't I worry?"

Ross blinked. Then a slow grin creased his cheeks. "My, how our meek little Serena has changed. I think Gideon's in for a surprise." He closed the door and gestured toward the graceful curving staircase. "I think I'll let him answer your question. I've done more than my share in this enterprise. Why don't you go up to your room. It's the same one you used last time. I'll tell him right away you want to see him."

"I want to see him *now*."

"He wants to see you too," Ross said soothingly. "Only the most urgent matter would have kept him from greeting you personally. As soon as he's finished his business he'll be right up. Okay?"

"No!" She turned and started up the stairs. "It's not okay. Nothing is okay." She glanced down at him over the oak bannister. "But I'm going to make damn sure it will be soon."

A faint smile tugged at his lips. "I bet you will."

Serena slammed the door of the bedroom and threw her shoulder bag on the chair by the door. She couldn't remember when she had been so furious. What the devil was happening here? When she had arrived she had been shaken, filled with painful nostalgia and . . . fear. This house, Ross, and, most of all, Gideon, were all tucked safely into the past. The vulnerable girl she had been that night was also in the past, and she had no desire for that girl ever to become real to her again. She had made many painful sacrifices to make sure those vulnerabilities didn't exist any longer.

She drew a deep breath and closed her eyes. She was probably getting upset for nothing. He had probably heard by chance she was coming back to Mariba and thought it would be pleasant to see her again. Ten years had passed and their night together was bound to be as dreamlike to him as it was to her. The autocratic manner in which he'd arranged their meeting was annoying, but surely not threatening, and he was evidently being quite helpful to Dane.

Her eyes flicked open with shock. How did he know Dane was her brother? She hadn't given him her last name. If he hadn't known her last name, how could he possibly know she was coming to Mariba? Again, she shivered with fear. What did she know about Gideon Brandt? Nothing. He was an enigma seen through the eyes of a child, a child in a state bordering on emotional collapse. This episode was very strange. Was Gideon obsessed?

She moved slowly to the single window across the room. Decorative wrought iron bars guarded the windows as in many Spanish homes. Had the bars been there when she had been here before? She couldn't remember. Then, Gideon had said something about screens and keeping out the "critters." Heavens, she was becoming paranoid. She refused to panic. There had to be some reasonable explanation. She would see Gideon, they would talk and exchanged reminiscences and then she would leave.

She heard a low murmur of voices and her gaze was drawn to the patio directly below her window. Sunlight glinted and then was captured in the crisp, tawny hair of the man standing just below her. Gideon. She felt a tiny shock. His back was to her, but she recognized him instantly. He was dressed casually, a white short-sleeved shirt, black jeans and boots, all emphasizing the tough leanness of his body. He was standing beside a tall, brown-haired young woman in a Dior suit; whose lush figure would have given Raquel Welch an inferiority complex. The woman smiled at Gideon with unmistakable intimacy as he helped her into the back of a long navy blue limousine.

Then he stepped back and his hand lifted in farewell as the limousine pulled away.

A faintly rueful smile curved Serena's lips when

she turned away from the window. So much for Gideon's being obsessed. Gideon's important "business" that had taken precedence over her arrival was far sexier than she would ever be. And the completion of the "transaction" had probably taken place in the bedroom, not the library. A man who had such women at his beck and call would have trouble remembering, much less harboring an obsession for, an inexperienced seventeen-year-old.

The knock on the door was impatient and the door swung open before she could answer.

Gideon stood in the doorway, his gaze sweeping over her with a hungry eagerness that stopped the breath in her throat. Then he smiled, the deep slashing dimples indenting his lean cheeks. It was exactly the same. Warmth and gentleness and sunlight.

"I'm sorry I made you wait." He came forward, his steps springy and charged with vitality. She had forgotten the way he walked, the impatience, the grace, the directness. "Something came up at the last minute and—" He stopped. "Lord, you're beautiful. I knew you would be. I've even seen pictures, but it's not the same."

"No?" She whispered. She hadn't really forgotten, she realized. She had buried the memories, but not erased them. Now she knew she had remembered everything about him, the drawling nuances of his voice, the way he raised his left eyebrow, those dimples. It was all coming back to her, flowing through her in an irresistible tide. It was crazy. She had known him for such a short time. No one could leave so deep an imprint in a few hours. She shook her head to clear it. "Pictures?"

"Not many. You're fairly publicity-shy, aren't you? The one in *Women's Wear Daily* was pretty good though." His fingers reached up to touch her hair, drawn back in a neat chignon. "This is pretty, but I like it better down. All this sophistication kind of intimidates me." He shook his head. "Funny. It never bothered me with any other woman, but in you, it scares the hell out of me."

She found herself smiling involuntarily at the boyish admission. "I'm not particularly sophisticated. I live a very simple life in a cottage in upstate New York. Most of the time I wear jeans and a ponytail. Your lifestyle is probably more sophisticated than mine." Her smile faded as she remembered the Dior-garbed sex symbol Gideon had just escorted to the limousine. She stepped back. "In every way." She met his eyes and said crisply, "Now what the hell is going on here?"

A flicker of disappointment crossed his face. "Wouldn't you rather discuss it over dinner? I have a French chef now." He smiled teasingly. "Or I can make you another omelet?"

She shook her head. "Now," she said crisply. "Right now."

He shrugged. "I was afraid you'd be a little upset. Okay, I wanted you here on Castellano. Well, that's not exactly true. I wanted you anywhere I could get you, but I figured on Castellano we'd have a better chance to get to know each other."

She stared at him, stunned. She spoke with great deliberation. "And may I ask what you did to get me here?"

He made a face. "You're not going to like it."

"I'm sure I'm not. I haven't liked one thing that's happened to me since I arrived here."

His expression betrayed mischievous thoughts. "I could work at changing that impression. I'm always ready to oblige a lady."

Then, as he saw her expression darken stormily, he sighed. "Oh, all right, I lured your brother from Monte Carlo to Mariba, and bribed the local *guardia* to arrest him on fake drug charges. It was the only way I could think to get you here."

"Is that all?"

"Well, I did make sure you wouldn't be able to leave by air or sea until I gave the word." He smiled crookedly. "The officials here are very easy to impress with bills of high denominations."

"I can't believe this. It's utterly outrageous. *Why*, for heaven's sake?"

"I didn't think you'd come if I invited you," he said simply. "I didn't find you until two years ago, but you could have found me anytime." He paused. "If you'd wanted to find me. But you didn't want to see me again, did you, Serena? Even after your husband died five years ago, you still didn't come back to me."

She felt an unreasonable surge of guilt. "There was no reason to come back. We were strangers, ships passing in the night. There was nothing to come back for."

He nodded. "And you would have given me that same bull if I'd come up to New York. It would have been a hell of a lot harder for me to pry you out of the pretty little foxhole you'd dug for yourself on your home ground." He smiled gently. "And I've always been one for the easy way."

"You won't find this way easy." Her eyes were blazing. "What makes you think you can do something like this? Did you grow bored with your little island chickadees and decide you wanted something new?"

"You're not new." His brown eyes twinkled. "Our relationship is over a decade old."

"This is *not* funny."

"I didn't say it was." He shook his head. "Sorry, but I can't seem to stop smiling. I'm so damn happy to see you."

She felt a melting sensation deep within her and instinctively braced against it, letting her exasperation and frustration smother it before it could damage the barriers she was frantically erecting between them. "I'm not glad to see you. I was grateful for your help that night but . . ."

"Easy," he said quietly. "Don't fight so hard. There's no use your tearing yourself apart like this. I knew you would shy away from me. I thought about it a long time before I decided this was the best way for us. If I'd found you right away, we wouldn't be having this problem. You wouldn't have had time to convince yourself that we didn't mean anything to each other."

"We don't mean anything to each other. We don't even *know* each other."

"That's why you're here, to finish what we started ten years ago. Do you remember what I said about the way we belong together? Well, that will be the core and we'll see if we can start a chain reaction.

Friendship, sex, learning all about each other—we've got it all ahead of us."

She drew a deep breath. "Listen, I'm going into town, and you're going to call that colonel and tell him to release Dane. Then Dane and I are going to leave Mariba."

He slowly shook his head. "Not until you give me my chance. I'll make a bargain with you. Give me a week. Not so much to ask, is it? Spend a week with me and I'll promise to let you and Dane leave Castellano."

She eyed him warily. "And that will be the end of it?"

He grinned. "No, then I'll follow you back to your foxhole and dig in beside you, but at least you'll be in your own backyard."

She threw up her hands. "What kind of bargain is that?"

"The only one I'm about to offer you." His smile faded. "Take it or leave it. Otherwise, Dane will continue to whoop it up at the Hotel Cartagena until he has a long gray beard, and you'll stay here as my guest until you change your mind." His expression was suddenly hard as flint. "I don't bluff, Serena. I don't like using muscle, but I know how to." He turned away. "Make yourself comfortable. Dinner is at eight. I'll see you then."

"I want dinner in my room," she said jerkily. "Prisoners aren't required to observe the social amenities."

He turned at the door. "Then *we'll* have dinner in your room," he said quietly. "The two of us. I thought you'd prefer to use Ross as a buffer, but I'd like nothing better than to be with you one-on-

one." He suddenly chuckled and tapped his chest. "In fact, I can't imagine anyone this one would rather be on. Do you have any idea how much I wanted you that night?"

Her eyes widened. "No. You acted—"

"Like a damn eunuch?" His mouth tilted in a lopsided grin. "I didn't think you were capable of coping with my libido as well as whatever was tearing you apart. Besides, you were just a kid." His voice lowered. "But you're not a child now, so you'd better start thinking about coping."

"And you're threatening to rape me?"

"Not on your life. You're going to want it as much as I do. Sex is going to be a hell of a lot of fun, once we get over our first anger and resentment."

"We? *I'm* the one who should be resentful. You have no right to be angry."

"Maybe I don't have the right, but I do." His lips tightened and something wild and primitive flared in his eyes. "I resent your marriage, I resent your belonging to another man, and I resent the fact that you did your damnedest to forget me. I've tried to reason it away, but it's still there. I've waited for a long time, and for most of that time I was as angry and frustrated with you as you are with me right now. I've been close to exploding so many times, it's become practically second nature with me. I *deserve* my chance, dammit." He opened the door with barely controlled violence. "And I'll do anything on earth to get it. I can't—" He broke off and drew a deep breath. "Cripes, I didn't mean to say any of that. I was just going to play it nice and easy. It's been too long."

"That's what I've been trying to tell you." Serena's voice was shaking slightly. Gideon's intensity had been electrifying, blazing out at her, enveloping her. Her memory of him had always been of gentle, glowing tenderness, not this fiery sensuality. "It's been too long. I'm not the same person."

He studied her thoughtfully. "I know you've changed, but that doesn't mean we can't be good together. It might even be . . ." He stopped and then asked abruptly, "Do you still paint?"

"Occasionally," she answered, surprised. "I don't have much time these days."

"You wanted to be an artist, yet you became a fashion designer." His eyes were narrowed on her face. "Why?"

"It was necessary." She shrugged. "I had a commercial talent that could be exploited. I'm very successful at what I do."

"I know. I'm just curious why the daughter of Countess Mara de Lâncombe and the stepdaughter of one of the richest men in England felt the need to make such a compromise." His gaze held her own and his lips curved in a bitter smile. "Your Italian husband had nothing to offer besides the title, from what I understand, but surely your mama and papa were willing to help."

"You know a great deal about me." Her gaze slid away from his.

"Not enough. That's one of the reasons you're here. Why didn't you ask them for help?"

"That's none of your business." Her now defiant gaze returned to him. "It's my life, and you have no part in it. Everyone has to make compromises. I just grew up."

"I see." There was a touch of sadness on his face. "You did it quite beautifully. I just wish I'd been around to watch you and help you out now and then. I would have liked that very much."

That same poignant melting occurred within her again, even stronger now. Just when she thought her resentment of his actions had drowned any spark of softness, he said something like this. "Gideon, don't— Let me go. None of this is going to do any good."

"We'll see. If not, it's back to the foxholes." He turned. "Eight o'clock. We'll dress for dinner. Downstairs or here? It's up to you."

The door shut behind him.

At seven-thirty Serena took a last look in the mirror. If sophistication could intimidate Gideon, then the lounging pajamas she had chosen to wear tonight would accomplish her purpose. The violet trousers were so full they could easily be mistaken for an evening skirt, and the matching loose tunic top of silk suggested rather than outlined her curves. However, the square neckline was so low it barely covered the tips of her breasts and the silver scrolled trim that bordered the neckline blatantly called attention to their swelling fullness. She had worn the outfit only once before, to a press party introducing her spring line, and brought it with her only because she might need its glittering sophistication to charm an official and help her spring Dane from jail. It was a little too revealing for her personal taste, but if it served now to prove to Gideon how much she had changed from the wide-eyed child he had known so briefly, so much the better. She slipped on a pair of high-heeled silver sandals, smoothed her chignon into sleek order, and nodded with satisfaction at her reflection. Confidence, elegance and sophistication were what she had targeted, and she had hit the bull's-eye.

Ross met her at the foot of the stairs, dressed in a dark blue tuxedo, and gave an admiring whistle, half beneath his breath. "Lovely." His gaze lingered on the swell of her breasts revealed by the tunic. "Not exactly safe, but lovely."

"It's very fashionable. I should know. I designed it myself," she said. Then, realizing how defensive she had sounded, she continued quickly, "Things around here have certainly changed." She gestured at the gleaming black and white tiles on the floor and then at the exquisite crystal chandelier lighting the foyer. "Aubusson carpets, a Ming vase in the upstairs hall, and your sartorial elegance. Do you always dress for dinner?"

He shook his head. "Hardly ever. We get too much of these monkey suits when we're on the job. No, this is strictly in your honor."

"On the job?"

"Gideon owns a chain of casinos and resort hotels throughout the Caribbean and the Bahamas. The largest one is on Santa Isabella, which is our home base now."

"Castellano isn't your base?"

Ross shook his head. "Gideon kept the house and his contacts on the island, but we haven't done any business here since the early days. Castellano is too unstable for Gideon's taste."

"I can't see Gideon as a tycoon."

"No? Talk to some of the people who have gone up against him sometime. Gideon is scrupulously honest, but that doesn't keep him from being a damn tough businessman." He waved his hand to a door to the left of the foyer. "Let's go into the library and I'll get you a drink. Gideon said he'd be a little late for dinner."

"More business?" she asked with the lightest of sarcasm.

He hesitated. "Yes, I guess you could call it that."

She had a fleeting memory of the voluptuous sensuality of the woman she had seen with Gideon. "I imagine you could call it a good many things." She sailed past Ross and entered the library.

An amused smile tugged at Ross's lips as he crossed to the cellarette on the far side of the room. "Do I detect a shade of annoyance in your tone? I gather Gideon wasn't able to pacify you."

"Did you really think he could?"

"No, but there was always a chance. Gideon can be very persuasive. What would you like? Wine, a highball?"

"White wine." Her eyes narrowed on him across the room. "Just how deeply are you involved in all this?"

"Up to my neck," he admitted as he poured wine into two fluted glasses. "Gideon did the ordering and I did the running. I lured Dane to Mariba with the promise of wine, women, and song." He moved across the room toward her. "I delivered on all three by the way. Dane is having one hell of a party at the hotel. You're going to have trouble getting him to leave Mariba."

"You placed him in a dangerous position with a government everyone in the world knows is corrupt."

"But they're not stupid, and they know better than to try to pull a fast one on Gideon. They learned a hell of a lot of respect for him before he pulled out of Castellano. The *guardia* will earn their bribe, or he'll take it out of their skins."

She shivered. The man Ross was talking about was completely alien to the man she had known. She took the glass he handed her and looked down into its clear golden depths. "The taxi driver called him 'The Texan.' He said it in capital letters, as if there were only one."

Ross shrugged. "It's a nickname he picked up when we first arrived here. You'll find out it's a sobriquet well-known in the Caribbean these days." He took a sip of wine. "And as far as this hemisphere is concerned, there is only one. You can't confuse him with anyone else."

"No, he's definitely an original," Serena said faintly. She lifted her glass to her lips. "Would you like to tell me why you helped him with this insanity?"

"I owed him," Ross said simply. "I helped you to get away from him. I thought I was doing the right thing, but it didn't turn out that way. He went crazy worrying about you. He tore Mariba apart, trying to find a clue to where you had gone. We finally decided you must have arrived by ship and left the same way."

Serena nodded. "I told you I had somewhere to go."

"And that you were married. I thought it might make a difference to Gideon." His lips twisted. "It didn't. He said if the bastard had sent you wandering the streets in such a state, he didn't deserve to keep you. So we started looking for you." He took another sip of wine. "As soon as the money started coming in he hired a detective agency. You didn't leave much of a trail and it took a long time. Two years ago they tracked you down."

"Two years." Her smile was faintly skeptical. "He wasn't overeager to resume our acquaintance. Perhaps he's more enthralled with the idea than the reality. I'm sure he's had plenty of distractions to amuse him."

"Women? He's a man. What did you expect?"

"Nothing. It's nothing to me if he has an entire harem. That's what I've been trying to tell you."

"I'm tempted to bring up the old chestnut about protesting too much," he said lightly. He checked his wrist watch. "It's almost eight-thirty. We'd better go into dinner. Gideon said not to wait for him, if he didn't show up."

"How considerate. He practically abducts me and then can't be bothered to show up for dinner. I don't believe he knows what he wants."

"Wrong." Gideon stood in the doorway. "I know exactly what I want, it's just that everything seems to be conspiring to keep me from getting it." He came forward, smoothing his rumpled hair with one hand. He was dressed in a black tuxedo and ruffled dress shirt and wore them with as much ease as he had jeans and boots. "Sorry to be late. I had an emergency and then I had to change again and—" He broke off, his gaze on the expanse of creamy flesh revealed by the neckline of Serena's tunic.

Serena felt the hot color rush to her cheeks. What was wrong with her? She couldn't remember when she'd blushed last. "It's rude to stare."

"Sometimes being a poor ignorant cowboy has its advantages." He hadn't taken his eyes off the deep cleavage swelling from the low bodice. "Unlike city dudes, when something is offered we reach out and take. If you hadn't wanted me to look, you wouldn't have put yourself on display like this." His gaze reluctantly moved up to her face. "Now, would you?"

"Of course I would. Low necklines are in this year, particularly the Elizabethan look. It's very stylish to—"

"Make a man want to drag you off to the nearest bed?" he finished softly.

"No, that isn't what I meant at all. Not everyone is—"

"I suggest we go into dinner," Ross interrupted quickly. He took Serena's glass and set it on the Sheraton desk behind him. "Gideon, leave her alone. She's been through enough today."

Gideon seemed mildly surprised. "My, how protective you're being. Maybe I shouldn't have left you alone for quite so long." Gideon's glance returned to Serena's breasts. "I sure as hell wouldn't, if I'd known she was going to pull an Eleanor of Aquitaine."

"Yes, you would." Ross's gaze searched Gideon's face. "Is everything okay?"

Gideon nodded. "Better. For now."

"Eleanor of Aquitaine?" Serena asked, bewildered.

"She rode bare-breasted at the head of her troops into the fray," Gideon told her solemnly. "Isn't that what you're doing, Serena? I've never seen a challenge more beautifully obvious."

"Dinner," Ross said again, taking Serena's arm and nudging her gently toward the door. "With all possible speed."

Serena heard Gideon's low chuckle behind her as Ross ushered her quickly from the room.

Two

The service at the table was provided by a slim, dark-skinned young man and was both quiet and unobtrusive. The crystal and china were exquisite, the food was a gourmet's delight. Serena was scarcely aware of any of it. She was conscious only of Gideon's gaze fixed on her with an intensity that caused the surroundings to fade.

Ross attempted the difficult task of keeping the conversational ball in the air, but received only monosyllabic replies from Gideon and Serena. When the meal was over he pushed back his chair, sighed in relief, and said, "Coffee in the study, I think. I hope you both realize I'm planning on nominating myself for a medal. I deserve it after submitting my sensitive psyche to the flak the two of you have been mentally tossing at each other."

"Flak?" Gideon raised an eyebrow. "That's a poor choice of words. I'm not feeling in the least warlike." He threw his napkin on the table and rose to his feet. "Though I admit my thoughts were definitely incendiary."

"I think it's a very fitting word," Serena said coolly. "I'm feeling extremely militant at the moment."

Gideon smiled. "Eleanor into the fray?" he asked softly. "I can hardly wait."

Serena found her gaze clinging to his as if she were mesmerized. She didn't know how many seconds passed before she was able to tear her glance away. She drew a deep breath and tried wildly to think of something to say to destroy the electricity charging the atmosphere between them. "I'm no Eleanor, and you'll wait a long time, Gideon."

"I already have." He grinned. "But at least I'm halfway home."

She frowned. "What are you talking about?"

"That night at Concepción's." His gaze teasingly lingered on her breasts. "It chafes my possessive instincts to know I wasn't the only one to be so privileged, but that memory has furnished me with a number of fantasies through the years."

The color flooded her cheeks as the memory of gentle hands pulling the white satin bodice up to cover her bare breast suddenly came back to her. "I forgot about that," she whispered.

His smile faded. "I think you tried to forget everything about me, didn't you? I wonder why you felt the need. We're going to have to discuss quite a few things, Serena. Do you remember the bushwhackers we talked about? I have an idea one of them got to you after you left me."

She suddenly felt unutterably weary. "Quite a

few of them got to me, but I fought them off the only way I could." She smiled with an effort. "And in the end I came out on top."

"Not entirely," he said slowly. "You let them take a few things away from you. I guess I'm going to have to see what I can do about getting that booty back."

Ross suddenly coughed. "Look, I'm still in the room," he said mildly. "I just thought I'd point it out, in case I'd become an invisible man."

Serena smiled vaguely at him and turned her attention back to Gideon. "The only thing I want you to get back for me is Dane."

"In time." Gideon's eyes narrowed. "I told you what my terms are. All you have to do is to agree, and I'll put the wheels in motion. Lord knows I want to give you whatever you want. Just give me my chance to—" He suddenly broke off as the slim, white-garbed young man who had served dinner appeared at his elbow. The boy murmured something in a low tone and then disappeared as quietly as he had come.

Gideon's expression was abstracted as he turned away. "Something's come up," he said tersely. "Take care of her, Ross." Then he was striding out of the room without giving Serena another glance.

"I gather I've become visible again," Ross said. "Coffee, Serena?"

"No." Her tone was also abstracted. It shouldn't have bothered her that Gideon was constantly relegating her to second place in his scheme of things. It shouldn't, but it did. She had felt as if she had been flicked with the stinging tip of a lash when he'd walked out the door. "I thought I'd go to my room. I'm sorry I was rude, Ross." She suddenly realized she was apologizing to Gideon's partner in crime, and scowled. "Though you both deserved a hell of a lot more than rudeness. Burning at the stake would be most appropriate."

"Whew, how fierce we are," he murmured. "I can't help it if Gideon was forced to opt out of the fireworks. Spare me your wrath, Queen Eleanor."

"And that joke is getting very old." She turned away. "I want to talk to Dane tonight before I go to bed. Will you give me the number at the hotel?"

He nodded, took out a business card and scrawled a number on the back. "Just ask for the Royal Suite." He grinned. "I told you we were taking good care of him."

Serena realized that was a gross understatement when she hung up the phone in her room an hour later. Dane was not only unconcerned about having to stay in Mariba for a good deal longer. He actually sounded reluctant to leave Castellano. She supposed she should be grateful that he wasn't depressed, but she was experiencing only frustration and exasperation. She could have used a little company worrying about their situation, dammit.

She stood up and strode across the room to the closet. She would shower and go to sleep and forget all about Dane and Gideon and the tangle she had to uncomb before she could return to her calm, controlled existence. She pulled her loose gray silk robe from the hanger and started to close the door. She froze.

It couldn't be. She reached into the back of the

closet and brought out the white satin nightgown she had tossed carelessly on the cane chair ten years ago. It shimmered, as pristine as if it were new.

She slowly hung the nightgown back on the rod and closed the door. The gown had brought back too many memories, not of Antonio and the horror of that night, but of Gideon and the way she had felt about him. She closed her eyes as she remembered the pain she had felt as she walked down the stairs and out of his life. Lord, she didn't want to recall the moment. Was that why he had left the blasted gown in the closet? It was a clever move and she was beginning to realize Gideon was a very clever man beneath his lazy cowboy facade. She opened her eyes, turned, and moved resolutely toward the door of the bathroom.

An hour later she had showered, had washed and blow-dried her hair, and felt a good deal more in control. She drew back the spread on the bed, plumped the pillows and then moved briskly to the window to open it wider.

Gideon was on the patio.

Serena froze. He was sitting on the rim of the mosaic-tiled fountain. He had discarded his jacket and tie and the sleeves of his ruffled dress shirt were rolled up to the elbow. The moonlight touched his hair with flecks of silver and gave his face a stark grimness. He was staring straight ahead, but she didn't believe he was seeing anything but the pictures flashing through his mind. What was he thinking to make him look like that? What emotions were . . .

He lifted his head.

Serena inhaled sharply as she saw his expression. Sadness. Terrible sadness and an aching loneliness. No, he shouldn't feel . . .

She turned impulsively and ran from the room and down the stairs. She had to do something. Gideon was hurting and she had to stop the pain. She *had* to stop him from hurting. It wasn't until she was standing only a few feet away from him on the patio that she realized how instinctive had been her action. Then all objective thought was gone again as he looked up and saw her.

His dark eyes were glittering in the moonlight. "Hello. I'm sorry I had to leave you tonight. Things just don't seem to be working out."

She took a step closer. "What's wrong, Gideon?"

"Death," he said simply. "I guess that's about the biggest wrong of all, isn't it? It's the one thing you can't fix, no matter how hard you try."

Serena felt an aching sympathy. "Do you want to talk about it?"

"It was Frank. I keep telling myself he was old and sick, that he'd lived a good life these last years at least. None of it does any good."

"Frank," she murmured. "I guess I assumed you'd found a home for him with someone else. Ross said you did that at times."

He shook his head. "I kept him with me wherever I went after we left Castellano. I . . . loved him."

Tears burned her eyes. "I think perhaps I loved him too. He helped me so much that night."

"Did you ever get a dog after you left me? I always wondered if you had."

"No. Like you, I moved around a lot. It wouldn't

have been fair to a pet. I kept my friend Eliza-
beth's dog for a while. He reminded me a little of
Frank." She took a step closer. "Were you with
Frank earlier this evening too?"

He nodded. "The vet thought he was out of
danger, but he had a relapse. He didn't last more
than an hour after I got back to him." He swallowed. "It hurt to watch him die."

"But you stayed with him."

He looked up in surprise. "Of course. Death is
lonely. I think it must help to have a friend there."

She reached out and gently touched his cheek.
"Anything is better, if you have a friend there."

He went still. "Is that an invitation?"

"I'd like to be your friend," she said simply. "In
a way, I think we're already friends, Gideon. I
can't give you what you seem to want from me,
but I can give you this. Let me help you." She
stepped into his arms as naturally as if she'd
never left them one night long ago. She could feel
him stiffen and then slowly relax against her.

"I'd be a fool to turn down your offer, wouldn't
I?" His arms tightened around her and his cheek
pressed against her temple. "Lord, I'm hurting,
Serena. You know, old Frank was a little like me. I
guess that was why I grew to love him so damn
much. We were both wanderers and had been
through the mill. We both had our scars."

Serena could feel a moistness on her temple
and she instinctively tightened her arms about
him.

"There were times when I was lonely or things
weren't going right but he was always there. He

was happy and affectionate and—" His voice broke. "—and loving."

"You told me that once," Serena said huskily. "You said he had toughened up, but kept the loving."

"Yes." He was silent a moment, just holding her. Then his arms dropped away from her and he stepped back. He reached into his back pocket and drew out his handkerchief. "I didn't mean to drown you." He dabbed at her temple, dampened by his tears, and then unashamedly wiped his own eyes. "But Frank deserved tears." He stuffed the handkerchief back into his pocket. "Thank you."

"For what?" She smiled at him. "I didn't even lend you my shirt or make you an omelet. We're still not even."

"This is no contest," Gideon said gravely. "Friendship makes no comparisons. It's just giving and taking. Thank you for giving."

"Thank you for taking. It was good to be needed. I don't think anyone has ever needed me before." She made a face. "Except Dane, and the only help he ever needs is rescue."

"No one?" Gideon asked. "Not even your husband?"

Her expression was suddenly shuttered. "No, Antonio never needed me." She stepped back. "I think it's time I went to my room. Why don't you go to bed, too?"

"Another invitation?" He held up his hand, a faint smile touching his lips. "No, I know comfort only extends so far and no further. I was joking." He wearily rubbed the back of his neck. "I think I will go to bed. One way and another, it's been a hell of a day."

"You could have eliminated one source of strain, if you hadn't practically kidnapped me," she said lightly. She was actually teasing about his treatment of her, she realized with astonishment. At some time on this patio tonight, anger and resentment had fled, and she wasn't sure she could ever summon them again to use against Gideon Brandt. She wasn't sure she even wanted to summon them. Being at peace with Gideon was filling her with a golden tranquility and warmth.

"I did what I had to do." His gaze was running over her. "I like that silvery robe. It makes you look like a moon maiden."

She laughed. "I thought moon maidens were probably made of green cheese too."

He tilted his head as if he were listening to music. "Lord, that's pretty. I've never heard you laugh before. I'm going to have to work on giving you more to laugh about." He laced his fingers through hers and started across the patio toward the front door. "Maybe I could hire a resident clown, or send for a joke book or—" He broke off. "But I'll need time to do all that." He gazed intently at her. "Am I going to get that time, Serena? Am I going to get my week?"

How could she refuse a man who would postpone initiating a plan he'd held for ten years to comfort a dying animal? A strong man who was not ashamed to show either tears or need. How was it possible to refuse Gideon Brandt?

"I'm very much afraid you are," she said huskily. "It's a mistake, but I'll give you your week. I don't know why. You've been completely autocratic and—"

"It's no mistake." A radiant smile lit his face. "I'll make sure it's the best decision you've ever made." His hand tightened around her own. "Damn, I'm glad."

She had made him happy. The knowledge sent a heady burst of exhilaration through her. He had been sad and she had given him happiness. What difference did a week make? Dane was completely happy where he was, and she had no commitments for the next few weeks. She owed Gideon far more for his past support than he had asked of her. "I'm not promising you anything more than friendship. I still think this is crazy and—"

"Hush, don't spoil it." He lifted her hand to his lips and kissed the palm lingeringly. She felt a warm tingle begin to spread from her palm into her veins and then into every part of her body. "Let me be happy."

"All right." Her voice was breathless. The night was suddenly crackling with the same electricity that had charged the dining room earlier in the evening. She could feel her heart start to pound and the temperature seemed ten degrees warmer than it had only a moment ago.

His clasp tightened around her wrist, and she knew he had felt her betraying leap of response. "For me?" he murmured. "Let's see what else I can . . ." His tongue gently stroked her palm, his thumb on her wrist monitoring her reaction. "You like that?"

She felt as if she had been jolted by lightning.

The lightest of intimacies, and yet she was trembling. "I think I'd better go upstairs now."

"In a minute." He moved his lips to the delicate blue veins of her wrist. His tongue moved lazily, teasingly on her flesh. "I can feel your heartbeat going crazy. You're very easy to arouse, love. I'm so lucky." He nipped her wrist with his teeth and she felt a jolt of heat flood her. "We're going to be so good together."

She hadn't expected this, she thought wildly. One moment she was only wanting to comfort, and the next she was experiencing a sensual pull stronger than any she had ever known before. "Maybe this isn't such a good idea."

"No, don't start backpedaling. You made me a promise." He was smiling again, and warmth melted the panic starting to rise within her. "And I'm holding you to it. We'll leave for Santa Isabella tomorrow morning."

"Santa Isabella? I thought we were going to stay here."

He shook his head. "Santa Isbella is as much of a home as I've ever had. I want you to get to know it." His lips twisted. "Besides, the atmosphere in Castellano right now isn't conducive to relaxation and I want you mellow. Very mellow." He tugged at a lock of her hair. "I want to hear you laugh again." He bent quickly and placed a sun-warm kiss on her lips and then straightened. "That wasn't so bad, was it? I'll guarantee we'll get better at it." He took her hand again and they covered the remaining yards to the front door in silence.

It was only when they were going up the stairs

that he spoke again. "You're barefoot. I didn't notice on the patio." He grinned. "Do you have a violent aversion to wearing shoes? Not that I object, you understand. You have very pretty feet and I like to look at them."

"I forgot about them. I saw you on the patio and—"

"You wanted to help me," he finished softly, his eyes very warm. "So you scurried to the rescue, bare feet and all."

There had been a moment on the patio when she would have walked barefoot on hot coals, if it could have taken away a portion of Gideon's pain. "As I said, I'm new at having someone need me. I reacted without thinking."

"Instinct," he said thoughtfully. "You came to me instinctively. Think about that tonight. You might learn something about yourself and about us, too, perhaps. I believe in instinct." They had reached the top of the stairs and he paused to look down at her. "Instinct made me know you belonged to me that night." He touched her cheek with a fingertip. "Sleep well. I'll see you in the morning, love."

She hesitated. "Will you be all right?"

He nodded, then smiled. "You could leave your door ajar in case I get ambushed. I like the idea of your being available to hold me like you did out there by the fountain."

"I don't think you'll need me. I'm not as experienced as you at shooting bushwhackers out of the saddle." She turned away. "Goodnight."

She could feel his gaze on her back as she walked quickly down the hall and opened the door to her room. A moment later she was in bed, her head awhirl with a wild confusion of thoughts. Why had she committed herself? It was crazy. *She* was crazy. She had been swayed like a tree in the wind by sympathy, remembrance, and the sensuality he had evoked so effortlessly. She knew he'd had no intention of arousing her to this extent. He had just been himself, Gideon, and that had been enough. Even now, lying here in an emotional turmoil she was conscious of a nagging anxiety. Was he lying in his room across the hall unhappy and lonely again? Surely he had been joking about the possibility that he might need her to help him get through this time. Still, he hadn't closed his door on her, when there had been a chance she might need him.

She lay there for many minutes staring into the darkness, trying to make a decision. Then she abandoned all reasoning as totally useless. She had half known what she was going to do from the beginning anyway. Maybe Gideon was right, and following instincts was best.

She slipped out of bed and ran across the room. She opened the door and left it ajar in unspoken welcome, a gesture of friendship and support. Then she ran back across the room, jumped into bed, and pulled up the covers. It was done, and she felt immeasurably better. She closed her eyes and was asleep a short time later.

Gideon had left his own door open and was lying in bed, waiting. It was only a chance. It was really too soon for her to offer him that kind of trust, but maybe . . .

Then he heard the soft click of Serena's door

opening and the slight rustle of the mattress as she returned to bed.

Gideon smiled into the darkness, turned over on his side, and shut his eyes. There was still a faint smile on his lips when he, too, fell deeply asleep.

"Somehow, I didn't expect a coffee plantation," Serena said as the driver of the limousine negotiated the gravel road leading to the large stone house on the top of the hill. "Ross said your largest hotel property was here on Santa Isabella and I guess I thought you'd live near your base of operations."

"I have a penthouse suite at the hotel and I stay there most of the time." Gideon waved to a khaki-clad man in one of the fields bordering the road. The dark-skinned man waved back, a brilliant white smile lighting his face. "That's Henry Delgado, my foreman. He runs the plantation for fifty percent of the profits, leaving me to be the gentleman farmer. It suits us both." He leaned back on the blue velour seat and stretched out his legs. "I was going to sell off the land and just keep the house and a few surrounding acres, but that could have disrupted the lives of the farmers who live on the property. So Henry and I came to our agreement."

"How long have you had the plantation?"

"Two years."

Her gaze flew back to his face.

He nodded slowly. "I decided I'd better try to have a home ready for you," he said softly. "The hotel is plush and modern, but it isn't a home. The detective's report said you preferred your lakeside cottage to an apartment in New York so I thought this would do as well." His eyes twinkled. "I even made sure it had a lake on the property fed by a real waterfall. It's completely private and I've ruled it out of bounds for anyone on the plantation. I'll show it to you this afternoon, if you like."

"That would be very nice," she murmured.

He frowned. "Now you've got to stop freezing up on me when I mention things like that. I bought this house for us, and I'm not going to pretend anything else."

"I don't know what to say. I can't imagine any man doing all this on the gamble that a woman he'd scarcely met might be *the* woman."

"You *are* the woman," he said simply. "It was no gamble."

She shook her head. "You're utterly impossible, do you know that?"

He grinned. "It's been mentioned a few times."

"I can imagine."

"You'll get accustomed to me." His voice lowered to a velvet softness. "I'll give you every opportunity to further your knowledge in every way possible."

Serena felt the heat ignite in her veins like tiny licking flames and she quickly looked away from him. The sensual emphasis was clear, but not presented aggressively. There was no reason for her sudden breathlessness. Gideon managed to keep her constantly off guard. There had been no hint of sexuality in his manner either this morning at breakfast or on the short flight from

Castellano to Santa Isbella. He had been charming, humorous, considerate, and almost avuncular. Yet now he was smiling at her with a sensuality that was as frank and bold as a red flag waving in the breeze. "I wish you wouldn't do that."

He didn't pretend to misunderstand. "I try to keep it down, but it slips out sometimes." He grimaced. "I know my wanting you makes you uneasy. I had no idea the brother-protector image I built to make you feel safe that night long ago would be reinforced every time you thought of me for the next ten years." His gaze slowly traveled over her from yellow silk blouse to white linen skirt, returning to linger on the thrust of her breasts against the silk of her blouse. He spoke very deliberately, in a tone too low for the driver to hear. "I'm still your protector, but not your brother. If I were your brother, my thoughts couldn't be more incestuous. At the moment, I'd like nothing better than to unbutton your blouse and take your breasts in my hands. I want to taste every part of your body. I want my fingers on you, around you, and in you. Every time I look at you my stomach knots and I get so aroused I'm hurting. If I weren't afraid you'd panic, I'd tell Ricardo to pull over and find a place in the bushes and do everything I've wanted to do to you for an eternity or so." He drew a harsh breath. "Do we understand each other now?"

She was staring at him, stunned by both the barrage of eroticism and its explosive effect on her. Heat was tingling in every vein, and her breasts, beneath his gaze, were swelling as if they were being stroked. She hurriedly glanced out the window. "Oh, yes, I understand."

She felt the warm solid weight of his hand on her knee and she inhaled sharply. She was trembling. She couldn't think, but was having no trouble feeling. Every nerve in her body seemed aflame and her muscles were turning as insubstantial as water. She kept her eyes fixed blindly on the passing scene outside the window as his hand gently rubbed her knee and then slowly pushed her skirt higher to skillfully massage her inner thigh with gentle fingertips. "No stockings," he murmured. "I thoroughly approve."

"It was hot." The words were barely audible and her gaze clung desperately to the passing coffee fields. She should stop him, but she didn't *want* to stop him. She wanted to sit here and let him touch her and be bathed in this sensual sorcery that was already bewitching her.

"Heat can be a terrible thing." He was widening her legs gently, and she suddenly felt terribly vulnerable. "It can rob you of breath." His fingers trailed further up her thigh. "It can make your muscles knot." His hand suddenly moved up to the apex of her thighs and settled there. She shuddered. She could feel the warm heaviness as if the scrap of material didn't exist. "It can cause you to hurt." He rubbed gently. "Can't it, Serena?"

He didn't wait for an answer. His hand was suddenly gone and he was pulling down her skirt. "Remember, every time I look at you I'm feeling that same heat." He added softly, "Just like you. You want me. Thank God for that."

"I'm a woman and I have the usual responses," Serena said. "You're a very attractive man."

"You're quibbling." His voice was impatient. "Look at me, dammit." His fingers were beneath her chin, forcing her to face him. "Now, *tell* me. You want me, right? Not just any attractive man. *Me.*"

His gaze was holding her own with irresistible force. "Why should I—" She broke off and answered him honestly. "Yes."

He expelled his breath in a long sigh of relief. "Whew, you had me scared for a minute."

"You certainly didn't show it," she said tartly. "I feel as if I've been run over by a steamroller."

He chuckled and released her chin. "I guess I can be a little aggressive on occasion. Just shrug it off and tell me to go to hell. That's what Ross does."

"Not very often, I bet."

"Now that I think about it, he hasn't done it for a long time."

"I imagine he gets tired of being flattened."

For an instant Gideon appeared uncertain, then thoughtful. "I suppose I'll have to see what I can do about that."

Serena threw back her head and laughed. "Here we go again."

His expression was indignant. "Why are you laughing?"

"I can just see you plumping and pumping to unflatten Ross. I think he'd prefer you to let him stay flattened."

"The easy way isn't always the best way and if

Ross needs—" His lips quirked. "You think I'm too pushy?"

"It has occurred to me."

"I'll try to tone it down." He added half beneath his breath, "On the unimportant things."

Serena chuckled and shook her head. "Hopeless."

The limousine had pulled up to the front porch of the two-story stone house and Gideon opened the door and got out. He helped her from the car and whispered in her ear, "Never. There's no one more hopeful than I am."

A hot shiver chased down her spine and she looked away from him to the wide stone porch that fronted the house. "This house looks very old. When was it built?"

"The turn of the century." His glance flew to her face. "You don't mind old houses? I had this one thoroughly restored, and installed all the modern conveniences. I just think old houses have a special ambience."

"I think so too. My friend, Elizabeth, owns an old mill that has a wonderfully warm atmosphere."

"Do you want it?" Gideon asked. "Shall I buy it for you?"

She looked at him in surprise. "She'd never sell it. It's her home."

"I'll find a way."

He probably would find one, if she didn't get him off the track. "Back off, steamroller, perhaps you didn't hear me. She's my friend, and you don't bulldoze friends into the ground." She sighed with exasperation. "Why are we even discussing this? We're talking as if we're going to be together for the next fifty years."

Gideon smiled with satisfaction. "We are, aren't we?" He took her elbow and they climbed the stone steps. "I like that."

"Well, I don't. One week, remember?"

"I remember," he murmured. "Do you like the leaded-glass casement windows? They didn't come with the original house but I thought they fit."

"I think they're beautiful."

A brilliant smile lit his face. "Good. You can change anything that doesn't appeal to you, but I think you'll like most of it." He looked over his shoulder at the driver. "Put the baggage upstairs, Ricardo. Then you can go back to the hotel." He turned to Serena. "I have a maid who comes in every day to clean and cook, but I told her to stay away while you were here. I didn't want her getting in our way, and I figured we could take care of ourselves for a week." He smiled. "There are always omelets. I even had the phone disconnected." He opened the front door. "Welcome home, love."

For Serena, "home" had always been a place to come back to after the frenetic pace of the fashion world, or one of Dane's wild adventures. She had thought she preferred that concept to one of roots and permanency. During the short tour of the house, it became clear that wasn't Gideon's idea of home at all. This was a house in which to grow and change, a house in which to have children, a house to absorb the joys and sorrows of the people who lived within its walls.

Though the furniture was light and airy as befitted the tropical climate, it breathed comfort and color and homeyness. The floors throughout the house were polished to a warm, earthy luster, and even the huge family kitchen combined microwave efficiency with old-world charm. The bedrooms on the second floor were equally charming: canopy beds, delicately tinted Aubusson rugs scattered over gleaming hardwood floors, copper-based lamps, and vases holding fresh flowers. Everything about the house spoke of loving care and comfort.

"It's lovely. I don't wonder you bought it," Serena said sincerely as she looked out the leaded-glass casement windows in the master bedroom at an incredibly beautiful view of the sea in the distance. "It's absolutely perfect."

Gideon smiled delightedly. "That's a relief." He opened the door to the hall with a touch of boyish impatience. "I hate to lure you away from any bedroom just on general principles, but there's still one room you haven't seen yet. Come on, it's right down the hall."

There was a touch of maternal indulgence in her smile as she followed Gideon. Her smile faded as he threw open the door of the room at the end of the hall. "A studio?" She stepped slowly into the room. An artist's studio, completely furnished with everything she could possibly need. Floor-to-ceiling windows allowed sunlight to flood in, and an easel and paints stood in the center of the small room.

"It's been waiting for you, Serena," Gideon said quietly.

She swallowed. "I told you I didn't paint much anymore. Just sketches for my work."

"That doesn't mean you can't begin again. It's

all here waiting for you. There are some wonderful views from this hill. The sea can be a thousand different colors at sunset and that lake I mentioned looks like something out of a science fiction novel, wreathed in morning mist. You could start some sketches this evening and—"

"You want me to *work* during the week I'm here?" Her eyes had widened in surprise. "Aren't you defeating your own purpose?"

"Maybe." His lips twisted. "But it's the perfect opportunity for you to start again. I told you I didn't like the idea of your being robbed of any of your dreams, and I'll be damned if I'll let it go on."

Serena felt the tears sting her eyes. What a touching thing to do. "One week won't help much," she said huskily. "I'm terribly rusty. I haven't actually painted since the first year of my marriage."

"It would be a start." He grinned. "I bet I get you hooked again."

There was no question he was going to try, and Serena felt a sudden thrill of fear. Painting had always been a heady addiction. That was the reason she had stopped when she'd been forced to take up designing to earn a living for Dane and herself. It was a passion that could dominate her life, and blow her present career to bits. "I don't think I'd better . . . There's not enough time to make it worthwhile."

Gideon's smile vanished. "You're frightened, aren't you? Grabbing onto a dream can be as scary as hell. It's much easier just to drift along with the current." He paused. "But you have to be all you can be, Serena. You have to grab every brass ring and try every road." He crossed the few steps between them to look gravely down into her eyes. His own eyes were deep and glowing and his voice took on tones of velvet persuasion. "This will be good for you, baby. Trust me."

She pulled her gaze away and laughed shakily. "This is *not* a glass of orange juice. You're steam-rolling again."

"This is one of the important things." He took her chin in his fingers and brought her gaze back to him. "Remember, you promised me a picture. You never painted that picture for me, Serena."

He was wrong. She had painted a dozen pic-tures for him the first year after she had left him. It had been her only relief during that hellish period. "Do you want me to do a mural for the living room wall?" she asked flippantly.

"No, just one picture, but I want my choice, so you'll have to provide me with a wide selection." He brushed the tip of her nose with his lips. "Landscapes, portraits . . ." He leered clowningly. "Nudes. I want it all." Something hot and smoky flickered in the depths of his eyes. "All."

"You're not going to let me out of this, are you?"

"Not on your life."

She stepped back, already experiencing the be-ginning of the creative excitement she had thought she had forgotten. A blank canvas, paints, a beau-tifully lush tropical countryside . . . Oh, Lord, she shouldn't give in to him. It was a mistake, but one she knew she was going to make anyway. In fact, she could scarcely wait to start. "You may be sorry. There's something you should know about me. Ross once told me that one of your primary characteristics was determination. Well, one of mine is total single-mindedness. Once I focus on something, I become obsessive and can't let go." She tried to smile. "Even if it rips me apart, I still can't let go."

He nodded resignedly, his gaze on the eagerness lighting her face. "I'll learn to live with it. The sketch books and pencils are on the shelf beneath that work table across the room. Why don't you grab what you need and take it to your room and change? I'd like to take you on a tour of the grounds before it gets dark, and you might want to make a few sketches, if something catches your eye."

"I'll do that." The excitement was growing as she moved quickly across the room to the table. She glanced back over her shoulder and smiled. "Thank you, Gideon."

"It's my pleasure." His smile held a touch of self-mockery as he turned away. "I hope. I'll knock on your door in fifteen minutes. Okay?"

"Uhhmm." She was examining the sketch books and pencils.

His smile deepened. "I'll make it forty-five minutes." He quietly closed the door, leaving her alone in the sunlit studio.

Three

"I think I've created a monster." Gideon shook his head mournfully as he pushed his chair away from the table after dinner. "You were in that studio from after dinner last night until three o'clock this morning. In the past three days you've scarcely poked your head out that door. How the hell do you expect me to seduce you, if I don't see you?"

"I warned you," Serena said with an impish grin. "You're right. The situation is entirely of your own creation. Besides, we've had meals together, we've done dishes together, we went for a walk the first day we came and we played cards . . ." She frowned. "When was that?"

"My presence obviously made a deep impression on you," Gideon said dryly. "I might just as well have been playing solitaire. Well, I've come to the end of my patience. The seduction begins immediately." He leaned back in his chair, stretched his legs in front of him, crossing them at the ankle. "And I'm not only demanding a three-day extension. I want your complete attention for at least five hours a day. I know that's asking a lot when your new love is so absorbing but—"

"You're jealous," said Serena, amazed. "You're actually jealous."

"You bet I am. I'm jealous of everything concerning you. I was jealous of that fancy prince you married; I was jealous of the years that separated us; now I'm jealous of a damn palette of paints."

"You handed me the palette of paints."

"And I'll hand them to you again—tomorrow." He made a face. "So much for my grand gesture."

"It was a grand gesture," Serena said softly. He had given her back something very precious that might have been lost forever, and he had given it with a touching generosity. He had not only let her absorb herself completely in her work, but he had deliberately rid his manner of any hint of sexuality during the last three days. She might as well have been living with an indulgent older brother. "And I think perhaps, you're a very grand man, Gideon."

"It was all a plot, you know, to create an impression. Now that I've set you up, I'm ready to move in for the kill." He stood up lithely. "Let's go for a walk."

"Where?"

"Down to the lake. That's where I'm going to make love to you."

Her eyes widened. "Now?"

"Nope. Right now I'm going through the mating rituals. Don't worry, I'll choose the right time."

Serena felt a prickle of annoyance. Gideon was running things again. She stood up and faced him. "No."

He blinked. "No?"

"You're not going to bulldoze me, Gideon." She placed her hands on her hips. "Let's get a few things straight. *If* I let you make love to me, it won't be seduction. It will be because I want to make love. And I'll be the one to choose the time." She turned and started from the kitchen. "Tonight you can do the dishes by yourself."

"Where are you going?"

She glanced back over her shoulder, "To my other lover." Then she suddenly smiled with loving sweetness. "By the way, I have every intention of giving you what you want . . . eventually." Then she was gone and a moment later he heard her steps on the stairs.

He stared blankly at the door until a slow smile containing both pride and a touch of mischief lit his features. "Well, I'll be damned."

She didn't look up from the canvas when she heard the door of the studio open a few hours later. "Gideon?"

"Uh-huh."

"I'll be through here in fifteen minutes or so. I have to get the shading at the foot of this tree right."

"I wouldn't think of disturbing you." His voice was silky. She heard his steps behind her. "You just keep right on painting."

"It will only be— What are you doing?"

"Nibbling your ear. Quite tasty." He stopped her with his hands on her shoulders when she would have turned around to face him. "No, your work is too important to postpone. You paint away, love. I'll find something to keep myself amused." His tongue suddenly plunged into her ear. "Your hand jumped. Now you'll have to take care of that little smudge, won't you? Sorry about that."

"I'm sure you are." She could hardly speak through the tightness of her throat. The clean smell of soap and a minty after-shave lotion was surrounding her, and his body was emitting a masculine heat as aphrodisiac as the pungent male scent of him. She tried to steady her brush. "You're making it very difficult."

"Am I?" His arms reached around her and his deft fingers began to unbutton her blouse. "Well, life can be tough sometimes." He spread the edges of her blouse back and unfastened the front catch of her bra. "We have to learn to overcome these little upsets. I'm sure if you concentrate, you can forget what I'm doing to you." His hands suddenly closed on her bare breasts. "Oh, now you've made another smudge. Maybe you should make those tree roots instead of shadows."

She swayed a little, her breasts lifting beneath his hands with every breath. "Gideon, don't . . ."

"You've got such sweet nipples. They're poking at my palms as if they're nuzzling against me." His voice was thick. "And the weight of these pretty things is driving me crazy." He pressed his hips against her and rubbed slowly back and forth. "See?"

His length was hard and aroused as he undulated against her, and his hands were squeezing her breasts rhythmically. "Do you know what I'd like to do to you? I'd like to take all these clothes off you and try a little painting myself. I'd paint your nipples scarlet." His hand moved down to the apex of her thighs and began to rub gently. "And this lovely thing a warm gold. I'd use a very soft, delicate brush, and I think you'd like it as much as I. I'd take a very long time and each stroke would be slow motion." His teeth bit lightly at her earlobe. "I'd make sure you felt every bristle of the brush as it dipped into every curve and valley. Do you think you'd moan as I did that, love? I'd love to hear you moan and pant. Then I'd wash it all off and use my own brush to stroke you and make you moan." He brought her in solid contact and held her there for an endless moment as he buried his lips in the nape of her neck. "I think you've dropped your brush."

"I don't care." She was trembling helplessly. "Let me turn around."

"Why?"

"I want to touch you." The words were so faint, they were almost inaudible. "This isn't fair, Gideon."

"I know, but it's a hell of a lot of fun."

"Not for me. I feel so helpless."

He hesitated and then his hands dropped away from her. "Touch me."

She turned and nestled against him. Her shaking fingers quickly unbuttoned his blue chambray shirt. Then she pushed the cloth aside, and pressed her naked breasts against his hair-roughened chest. He gasped and she could feel the shudder running through him. She didn't seem to have the breath to gasp. Her lungs were so starved for oxygen that they felt as if they were burning up. She couldn't seem to get close enough to him. She wasn't conscious of the low sound of hunger she made as she thrust her breasts against him, rubbing the sensitive nipples into the springy thatch of thick brown hair that roughened his tanned chest. The fiery friction made her cry out again.

"Easy." Gideon's voice was a choked murmur. "I want it as much as you do, but if we're not careful I'll just lift you up and take you right here."

"Okay." Her voice was muffled. "Anywhere."

"The lake." He was breathing harshly, his chest lifting and falling against her lips.

"It's too far."

He pushed her away. "It will give us time to cool down. I want this to last a long time, love. You go change into that violet thing you wore the first night and I'll get a blanket."

"That's an evening outfit," she said, bewildered.

"It doesn't matter. I want this to be special. Something to remember." He smiled beguilingly. "Please."

She stared at him helplessly. She was practically exploding and so was he, and yet he wanted to *delay* it? She opened her lips to protest, but that blasted smile was her undoing. Sunlit tenderness and little-boy pleading.

"All right." She turned to the door. "It's crazy, but okay. But let's *hurry*, dammit."

"Right." He ran by her and tossed back over his shoulder, "Downstairs in five minutes."

When they met in the foyer, Gideon had a quilt over one arm and an armful of towels in the other.

"Towels?" she asked. "We're going for a swim? I must have missed something along the way. That wasn't exactly the activity I had in mind."

He laughed with a joyous exuberance that caused Serena's exasperation to ebb away. "Neither do I, love. That's why we've got to hurry or I might be tempted to throw you down in the bushes and ravish you. The swim is afterward." He took her elbow and ushered her out onto the porch and down the steps.

The night was warm and balmy and heavy with the scent of jasmine and coffee beans, and Serena's silver heels sunk into the soft earth as she kept pace with his swift steps. She began to laugh helplessly. She felt young and crazy and more exhilarated than she had in years. "Gideon, this is absolutely insane. There are beds galore back in the house, and you opt for nature in the raw."

"I want everything perfect for you. The first time I saw the lake I knew I wanted to make magic with you there."

"Magic?"

"Lovemaking *is* magic when it's between the right people. I don't know what kind of relationship you had with your husband, but this is going to be better." His voice was suddenly fierce. "I'll make damn sure it's better. I'll wipe him out of your mind, if it takes a lifetime."

"Gideon . . ." She drew a deep breath. "I'm not about to make comparisons. You're probably the one who'll find me inadequate." She paused and then continued in a little rush, "I'm not very experienced."

He didn't reply for a moment. "I know you haven't had any lovers in the last two years. If there had been anyone on the horizon, I would have dropped everything and moved in right away." His gaze narrowed on her face. "Antonio?"

"There were . . . problems." She smiled with an effort. "Do we have to talk about this? I just thought you should know I don't have all the techniques down pat. I didn't want you to be disappointed."

He threw back his head and laughed joyously. "Disappointed? I feel like flying over the moon. Do you know how jealous I've been of that bastard?" His hand tightened on her elbow and suddenly they were almost running. "There aren't any techniques, only instinct, and we both have an abundance of that, don't we, love?"

Her spirits rebounded to reflect the same joy she could feel in Gideon. "I'll say we do."

They came out of the encircling palms into a clearing and Serena caught her breath. It was such an incredibly enchanting sight. In the moonlight the waterfall tumbling over the limestone rocks was a shimmering iridescent stream of silver as it poured into the onyx mirror of the pool. The dark encircling palms enclosed and imprisoned the jewellike beauty with a jealous intimacy.

She stopped on the moss-covered bank, mesmerized by the sheer beauty of the scene. "It's utterly fantastic," she said breathlessly. "I've never seen anything so lovely."

"Well, you can't paint it. Not tonight, at least." Gideon dropped the towels on the ground and then spread the quilt with a quick billow of material. He turned to face her. "Lord, you're beautiful. I knew when I first saw you in that outfit that I wanted to see you wear it here." He took a step, and one finger traced the silver-scrolled trim bordering the square neckline. "This shines in the moonlight, just like I knew it would."

She could feel the warmth of his finger on her breast through the thin material. "I thought you didn't like it. Eleanor of Aquitaine, remember?"

"I like it. I was just jealous of all the other men who had probably seen you in it." His gaze was fixed intently on the naked swell of her breasts above the neckline. "And I was trying like hell to keep from doing this." His hands slowly moved behind her and loosened the back zipper. Then he pulled the neckline down, baring her breasts completely. The silver banded bodice kept them high and saucy in the moonlight, the pale globes a voluptuous invitation. "Beautiful." His voice was harsh and thick and his eyes blazing hotly as they looked at her. "But it can be improved."

He slowly lowered his head and his tongue flicked teasingly at the nipple and then enclosed it in his mouth, suckling strongly.

Serena cried out, arching mindlessly toward him. She couldn't breathe. Her bones were melting. The entire world was melting.

His mouth moved to the other breast but his hand remained on the one he had abandoned, plucking at her nipple with thumb and finger. His lips left her and he took a step backward. He was breathing heavily and his eyes were smoky with need as he looked down at his handiwork. "That's what I wanted to see. Pointed, glistening, *mine*." He pulled her close, rubbing her newly aroused breasts against his chest.

The springy hair teased her unbearably and she shivered. "I can't take much more," she whispered. Her nails dug into his shoulder as his hips moved to brush her with his heated arousal. "Gideon . . ."

"I can't either." His voice was choked. "I wanted to go slow, but I can't . . ." His hands were fumbling for the bottom of the tunic and he stepped back to pull it over her head with one swift movement.

He unfastened the closure of the silk trousers and dropped to his knees before her. He hooked his thumb in the waistband and slowly pulled the silk down over her hips. As her naked flesh came into view he chuckled, "You're ready for me."

"This outfit was your idea. *I* was in a hurry." She felt his lips on the tender flesh of her belly and swayed helplessly. The soft breeze was touching her breasts and Gideon's lips were an even more maddening arousal.

His warm palm was suddenly cupping her, his thumb toying with the tight curls surrounding her womanhood. "Damn, you're sweet here. I want to play and . . ." His lips brushed her. Searing heat. She cried out and swayed toward him. His head lifted. "It's too late. I've got to have you now."

America's most popular, most compelling romance novels...

Here, at last...love stories that really involve you!
Fresh, finely crafted novels with story lines so
believable you'll feel you're actually living them!
Characters you can relate to...exciting places to
visit...unexpected plot twists...all in all, exciting
romances that satisfy your mind and delight
your heart.

EXAMINE 4 LOVESWEPT NOVELS FOR

15 Days FREE!

To introduce you to this fabulous service, you'll get four brand-
new Loveswept releases not yet in the bookstores. These four
exciting new titles are yours to examine for 15 days without
obligation to buy. Keep them if you wish for just $9.95 plus
postage and handling and any applicable sales tax.

☐ **YES,** please send me four new romances for a 15-day
FREE examination. If I keep them, I will pay just $9.95 plus
postage and handling and any applicable sales tax and you will
enter my name on your preferred customer list to receive all four
new Loveswept novels published each month *before* they are
released to the bookstores—always on the same 15-day free
examination basis.

20123

Name_____

Address_____

City_____

State_____ Zip_____

My Guarantee: I am never required to buy any shipment unless I
wish. I may preview each shipment for 15 days. If I don't want it, I
simply return the shipment within 15 days and owe nothing for it.

R 123

Now you can be sure you'll never, ever miss a single Loveswept title by enrolling in our special reader's home delivery service. A service that will bring all four new Loveswept romances published every month into your home—and deliver them to you before they appear in the bookstores!

Examine 4 Loveswept Novels for

15 days FREE!

(SEE OTHER SIDE FOR DETAILS)

"Thank heavens." Serena stepped out of the silk pajama bottoms and slipped off her sandals. Then she sat down on the blanket and watched him as he stripped. She felt no embarrassment at her total nudity. It was as if she had sat waiting for him to come to her a thousand times before. Her gaze ran over him in primitive enjoyment. Gideon was beautiful. Slim and yet sleekly muscled, his broad shoulders speaking of power and masculine strength. His buttocks were tight as a spring and his thighs a work of art. She would like to paint him someday, she thought dreamily, but not now. Now she only wanted to touch him, run her hands over those smooth muscles, and have him touch her.

Then he was beside her, his face darkly intense, as his fingers moved to her hair, fastening in its flowing silkiness as he pushed her back on the blanket. "I'll be slow later," he said thickly. "I promise, love, but I have to get inside you. It's like a fever, I'm hurting so."

"So am I." She opened her thighs and he moved between them. Then she could see only his face above her, flushed and heavy with sensuality, beautiful. A warm nuzzling demand at the heart of her womanhood and then his lips were covering her own.

He plunged deep and his lips covered the little cry she made. Hot. Slick. Full.

"Tight," he murmured. "Lord, you feel wonderful."

"So do you." She could barely speak. The exquisite fullness of him was pervading her entire body.

She wanted it to go on forever. Her hands closed on his shoulders. "Don't move. It's . . ."

He stayed like that for an endless moment. "I can't stand it, love." He flexed hungrily. "I *have* to *move*."

"All right. It's just—" She broke off as he began pistonlike strokes, driving with an explosive passion that almost tore her apart. She arched up, trying to help him, wanting more of him.

His fingers tightened in her hair and the slight pain was as erotic as the hot rhythm between her thighs. But the tension was mounting swiftly, too swiftly. "Gideon, it's too—"

"I know," he gritted the words between his teeth. "And I can't stop. It's been too long." He plunged deep and was still. He closed his eyes. "I want to stay in you forever." Then he was driving with a wild ferocity that shook them both to their foundations. The tension grew, spiraled, and then exploded into a brilliant release of beauty and rapture.

He collapsed on top of her, his chest moving harshly with his labored breathing.

"Damn, wasn't that wonderful?" He lifted his head and looked down at her. "Mine. You're mine now. I told you we belonged together." He kissed her with loving affection. "Don't you feel it, love? Why don't you admit I was right all along and we were meant to live happily ever after?"

Her breath was still coming in little gasps and her heart hadn't steadied its wild pounding, but she had to laugh helplessly up at him. "Gideon, don't you ever give up? This is taking unfair advantage of my vulnerable situation."

His eyes twinkled. "Oh, do you feel vulnerable?

Now I wonder why?" He stirred lazily within her. "Of course, I guess certain important strongholds have been invaded." His hands released her hair and reached down to cup her breasts. "And certain outposts have totally surrendered, but I can't see why you should feel vulnerable." The stirring was no longer lazy, but demanding. "I think maybe I'm going to see if I can make you feel that way again."

She inhaled sharply as his lips closed on her breast, and his teeth nibbled delicately. "I didn't think . . . not so soon."

"I didn't either. I believe I'm starving. I can't get enough." His head lifted and he looked down at her. "I may never get enough of you."

He began to move and Serena realized she might never get enough of Gideon either.

The brush of Gideon's lips against her cheek was as velvet soft as the warm glance of the sun. Strange that she should recognize his touch even in this state of half waking, she thought drowsily, as she turned her cheek to invite more than a light caress. It was as if she had known the touch and feel of him for a millennium of intimacy rather than a few short hours. Even if she were blind and deaf she'd know him by that gentle touch alone.

"Open your eyes, love."

Her heavy lids lifted to see him bending over her, his dark eyes warm and intent. She lifted a lazy hand to stroke the crescent creases in his lean cheek. "Is it morning?"

"No." He turned his head to capture her fingers with his lips, nibbling at the tips for a delicious moment before releasing them. "But I'm lonely. I need your undivided attention for a while."

She chuckled, as her arms slid over his naked shoulders. "You've had my undivided attention for more times than I can count tonight. But I'm always ready to oblige." Her tongue brushed the hollow under his shoulder blade. He tasted good. Salty and strong and alive.

"I'm not quite the satyr you think me, you insatiable wench," he said as he settled back on the pillows and pulled her back into his arms, cradling her dark head in the hollow of the shoulder she'd just caressed. "You don't appreciate the fact that I'm a very sensitive fellow. I have other needs besides the purely physical, you know."

"I hadn't noticed," she said teasingly, one hand moving to play lazily with the soft thatch of hair on his chest. This hair was sun-streaked, just like the rumpled lock hanging down on his forehead, she noticed idly. "You must admit you haven't been displaying much of your soulful side tonight. It was only natural for me to assume that you wanted more of the same." She raised her head to look down at him, the silken veil of her dark hair brushing his chest. "By all means, bare your sensitive soul. I'm waiting with bated breath." Then, as she saw the flicker of disappointment in the depths of his eyes, she sobered abruptly. Obviously he had been sincere, not teasing. She bent swiftly and kissed him with infinite gentleness. "Tell me," she urged softly.

He shook his head. "I didn't have any melodramatic declarations in mind. I just wanted to see you wake up in my bed, in my arms and to hold you. That's all."

Serena felt her throat tighten and she lowered her head to its former place on his shoulder. Those simple words had moved her unbearably. Her eyes were misting as they lay there in silent intimacy. Everything around them seemed to take on an added poignancy. The airy canopy above their heads, the gleam of the leaded-glass windows across the room, the glow of the copper lamp on the bedside table that Gideon had turned on when they'd come back from the lake. This place. This time. Could anything be more perfect?

Gideon's hand was stroking the fine hair at her temple and his voice was a deep rumble beneath her ear. "You know, when I was a teenager, moving from place to place, I used to want something totally my own, something beautiful that wouldn't change no matter what happened in the world around me." One finger moved down to outline her lower lip with a gossamer touch. "I guess it made me pretty much of a pain for a while. I was so damn possessive that I couldn't have any friends without wanting to be everything to them." His lips brushed the top of her head. "I learned my lesson eventually, when I found I was driving people away just when I wanted them closer. You can't force people to open their minds and hearts and take you in. You've got to be invited." His voice was husky as he continued haltingly, "I guess what I'm trying to say is that you might have to back off and shove me away if I come too close and try to barge in where I'm not wanted. You were right when you said I was pushy." His fingers touched her lashes that were now star-spiked with tears. "You see, I've found my something beautiful, and I might not want to let go, even for a little while. Not even to let you breathe and grow. You'll have to let me know, Serena."

Her chest was aching with every breath she took, as her arms tightened around him with almost maternal fierceness. She was hurting with everything that was in her for the child he had been, for the pain and loneliness of his past, for the hard lessons he had learned, and for the honesty and vulnerability of the man he had become.

The brimming tears now flowed down her cheeks, and she felt him tense against her as a drop dampened his shoulder where her head was resting. "Hey." He raised his head to look into her eyes. "What are the tears for?"

"Nothing. I've just decided I like the idea of having a pushy man around."

His gaze searched her face. "Forever?"

She went still. Panic and rejection rose within her. It was insane. Gideon was everything beautiful and good in the world. Why was she so terrified of making a commitment?

A flicker of disappointment crossed his face. "It's all right. I don't have to have the words right now. What happened tonight was in the nature of a promise anyway. It's good enough to last us for quite a while."

Yes, it was, she thought dreamily. They lay there a long time and gradually Gideon's arms relaxed about her until they were only a comforting possessive shelter to keep out the outside world.

She was almost asleep when his voice reverberated beneath her ear with a satiny hint of threat and with a gravity that made the words a vow. "But if you ever *could* bring yourself to say forever, love, I'd make sure you never regretted it. Not for a minute."

Four

"Sit still," Serene ordered as her charcoal pencil traced the line of the strong masculine column of his thigh. It was a beautiful line, she thought absently, graceful and symmetrical while remaining totally masculine. "How do you expect me to get this right if you're always moving?"

"I'm chilly," Gideon said plaintively. He stretched lazily, his sleek muscles rippling, before resuming the pose she required of him. "You can't expect a man to pose in the altogether without getting goosebumps, love."

"It's nearly eighty degrees," she reminded him heartlessly. The waterfall in the background should turn out very well and add to the primitive beauty of the picture. "If you weren't so tanned, I'd worry about your getting a sunburn."

He thought for a while. "Well, then, I think I'm much too modest to pose in the nude." At her distinctly derisive snort he gave her a sly glance.

"First, you ravish my magnificent virile body, and then you make me display my manly beauty for your lascivious pleasure."

She looked up indignantly. "You speak as if I'm making dirty pictures. This is art!" Then as she met the mischievous twinkle in his brown eyes, she said reprovingly, "Now, if you've finally run out of excuses, I'd appreciate it if you'd be still. Getting me hooked again was your idea, and you're the one who demanded a selection of paintings from which to choose. I've got to have a model, haven't I?" She sighed. "You're not much, but I guess you'll have to do."

"I'd better." The grin disappeared and he growled. "Because if you think I'm going to let you leer at any other naked man, you can forget it."

"I do not leer. I'm an artist, not a voyeur." She scowled. "I'm almost finished. Will you just be still for another ten minutes?"

"Unless I can think of another excuse."

She would *not* smile at him. The scamp needed only the slightest encouragement and he'd turn on the voltage that melted her resistance like hot wax. She wanted to get this sketch done.

It seemed he was actually going to let her do it, for he was quiet for the next several minutes while her pencil flew over the sketch pad. Strange how close they'd become in such a short time. She was perfectly at ease with Gideon in a thousand ways, both mental and physical. Though perhaps Gideon was right when he said they had had a head start because of the sense of belonging that had been a salient element of their relationship since the very first night together long ago.

How wonderful to have a lover who was also a friend, she thought dreamily. The passion that had seared them with its lovely flame had not precluded the warm glowing embers of companionship. Though an outrageous amount of their time together was spent experimenting with the physical delight they both found so intoxicating, there had still been time for the exploration of thoughts and personality.

"Serena?"

She didn't look up. "Yes?"

"I've come up with another excuse."

"I thought you would." She sighed. "What is it this time?"

"I'm horny."

She glanced up. "So you are," she said calmly, her lips twitching. "Nice of you to provide me with additional material for my sketch. Of course, to do it justice will take another minute."

"*One* minute." He was rising to his feet. "That's it! I've stood all I can from you, wench. First, you use me and then you insult me." He was beside her, tumbling her to the grass and mounting her supine body with lightning swiftness. He pinned her arms above her head and gazed down at her laughing face with mock ferocity. "I think I'll have to ask you to reassess your opinion." He shook his head mournfully. "One minute. You really know how to hurt a guy."

"Well, maybe, two," she said grudgingly, trying to stop laughing. It was evident her sketching was finished for the afternoon. Then, as she felt the warm, hard length of him against her belly, her breath caught in her throat. "Yes, definitely two."

"Thanks," he said with irony. "But that's not good enough. I believe drastic action is definitely called for." His eyes were suddenly dancing with devilment. "Very drastic." With one lithe movement he was off her, and then she was scooped up into his arms as he rose to his feet.

She clutched wildly at his shoulders. "Gideon, what are you doing?"

"We're going for a swim." He crossed the few yards that separated them from the lake. "I think I need to cool down a bit if I'm going to exhibit my stamina."

"You may be naked but I still have my clothes on," she cried, holding onto his shoulders desperately.

"Only shorts and that little bit of shirt. They'll dry in a jiffy in the sun."

She had no time to answer as he stepped off the bank into the cold waters of the lake.

"Gideon!"

"In a few minutes it will seem as warm as bathwater." He struck out with a lazy sidestroke in the general direction of the waterfall, propelling her with easy strength. "Relax and leave everything to me."

She had little choice in the matter, she thought wryly as her arms curved around his neck and she obediently relaxed against him. "Warm as bathwater, my foot."

But soon they were in the outer spray of the falls and she found Gideon was right; the water no longer seemed too cool on her warm flesh. It was shallow enough here for Gideon to stand upright, the water coming barely to his shoulders. He looped his arms loosely about her waist to keep her level with him. His hair was deepened to dark brown by the spray and clung to his head like a gleaming helmet.

Her fingers reached up to delicately trace the cool, damp contours of his cheek. "I can't get that line quite right. The bones are broader than you'd think at first glance." Her fingers wandered down his cheek. "And, of course, those dimples are utterly impossible."

"Sorry," he said automatically, before scowling crossly. "They are *not* dimples, they're laugh lines. Shirley Temple had dimples. *I* have laugh lines."

She snuggled closer. "I believe I've struck a nerve." She poked at a long dimple with her forefinger. "You shouldn't be so defensive. I think they're perfectly sweet." She leaned forward and her tongue licked teasingly at the crescent line. "Gideon's darling dimples."

"Nauseating," he pronounced. "You're piling up the score for retribution, woman." One hand left her waist to go to the buttons of her pink sun top. "Do you know the definition of a dimple?"

"I don't believe I do," she said warily.

"I do." He stripped the shirt from her and tossed it on a large boulder by the waterfall. "It's permanently engraved on my memory. I looked it up when I was a kid." He scowled. "After I bloodied the nose of the first boy dumb enough to call me 'Dimples.'" His hand was at the fastening of her shorts now. "A dimple is a natural hollow on the body, usually small, but not necessarily."

"What an interesting bit of trivia," she said breathlessly. Her breasts were brushing against the hard cool wall of his chest and she could feel them tauten, their sensitive tips beginning to blossom.

"I thought you'd be fascinated." Gideon slipped her shorts down over her hips. "But it's not trivia. I consider it a matter of some importance that everyone has dimples." The shorts slid down her legs and she kicked out of them. She really should try to keep them from floating away, she thought hazily, but at the moment it didn't seem very important.

"Some dimples are in the most enchanting places." He pressed her close and they melted together in magic alchemy. His hand went caressingly to one pert cheek of her buttocks. "There's a cute little one, right here."

"I never noticed."

"I did," Gideon whispered. "I notice everything about you." His lips touched hers in a kiss as light as fairy dust. "Do you know that you look fantastic under a waterfall? The spray covers you with diamond dew drops."

"How romantic," she said lightly, her throat tightening. "As a beauty aid it's hardly portable, however."

"I am romantic when I'm with you." Suddenly he was no longer laughing. "I want to tilt windmills and fight dragons for you. I'd like to write a song like the old troubadours did for their ladies and sing it under your window." His hand gently caressed the sleek glossy darkness of her hair.

"You know that commitment we were talking about?"

She stiffened unconsciously in his arms. Not now. Please, not now. "Commitment?"

He nodded, one finger tenderly brushing her wet lashes. "It's damn important, Serena. And there's no way I'm going to let you run away from it."

She didn't want to think about anything but him at this lovely moment. It had been such a wonderful three days. Why did Gideon have to interject this disturbing note now?

"Who's running?" she asked, deliberately pressing closer to him and rubbing her breasts against him in teasing provocation. "I'm standing still." She made a face. "For all the good it's doing me. I thought you were going to tell me more about my enchanting dimples."

A shadow darkened his face for a brief instant, and she saw a flicker of disappointment in the depths of his eyes. Then it was gone and his grin was as mischievous as ever. "Oh, yes, those dimples. I was about to go into that," he drawled. He made a slight adjustment in his stance, his hands lifting her legs so they curled around his waist. "Very deeply into that."

Her laughter was abruptly cut off and she inhaled sharply. Her fingers bit into the sleek, cool flesh of his shoulders as he suited his actions to his words.

She closed her eyes as he started to move with a forceful tempo, gradually escalating into world-shaking explosiveness. She could feel his heart pounding as erratically as her own and there seemed to be an element of driving ruthlessness about his thrusts that had been absent before. Ruthlessness? Gideon had never displayed anything but magical gentleness in his lovemaking. Yet there was undoubtedly a disturbing element, almost an anger in his possession now. No, she must be mistaken. For when they reached the climax of feeling that had become as necessary to her as water in the desert, his arms still held her with the same caring protectiveness as they always did.

His voice was the same, too, a husky growl with an underlying thread of humor. "*Two* minutes?"

Her answering laughter was lost in the mellifluous roar of the waterfall.

Still, there was unmistakably an air of abstraction in Gideon's demeanor as they retrieved her blouse and finally, after several dives, managed to find her shorts. It continued as they swam back to the bank and dressed before gathering Serena's sketch pad and pencils and setting off for the house.

She shivered as she cast a glance at the sky, which had darkened from cerulean blue to dull pewter while they had been in the water. "So much for my clothes drying in a few minutes," she commented. "We'll be lucky if we don't get drenched again before we get back to the house."

"What?" He glanced up at the thunderclouds gathering on the horizon. "Looks like rain. Let's get you inside."

His hand cupped her elbow and his pace quickened to a jog. By the time they reached the house, the threatening storm had become a reality. They ran the last few yards through a cloudburst.

"You'd better take a hot bath and get into some dry clothes," Gideon said quietly as soon as the door closed behind them. He was striding swiftly down the hall toward the kitchen. "I'll start a pot of coffee and put steaks in the broiler."

Frowning, she stood in the foyer looking after him. There was definitely something wrong. Any other time there would have been no question they would shower together, then share the kitchen tasks. "You're just as wet as I am," she called to him.

"I'm fine," he tossed over his shoulder. "Run along."

The casual dismissal shouldn't have bothered her, she assured herself firmly. Perhaps Gideon was growing tired of doing everything together. It was only natural for a man as independent as Gideon to chafe at constant invasion of his privacy. Just because she was beginning to find every moment spent without him lonely, she mustn't expect him to feel the same way. Yet the nagging uneasiness she was experiencing had a definite tinge of unhappiness as she turned and walked slowly up the stairs.

The uneasiness manifested itself in the extra care she took with her appearance. After her shower she reached for a rose and gold caftan instead of more informal wear. She put her hair up in a loose knot on her head, leaving a few wisps to curl around her face. A bit of powder and mascara, a touch of lip gloss, and she was ready to confront Gideon. She made a face at herself in the mirror. *Confront* Gideon? Why had those words occurred to her? They made him sound more like an enemy than a lover. Her imagination was really running away with her.

When she appeared in the kitchen a few minutes later she knew her elaborate toilette had been for nothing. Gideon glanced up casually as he put foil-wrapped French bread in the oven. "The steaks are almost done. I left the salad for you to do. I'll be with you in ten minutes." He left the kitchen.

She was frowning as she opened the refrigerator door and began to take out vegetables to make a salad. She might as well have been a post for all the attention he had paid her. Perhaps he *was* becoming a little bored. Well, she had all evening to pierce his wall of indifference.

She glanced out the window over the sink at the rain battering against the windows in sheets, an occasional rumble of thunder indicating that the storm would be around for some time. It was almost dark and she could barely make out the trees and shrubbery of the garden being buffeted by the wind. The idea of a storm coming at this particular time to disturb the sunny tranquillity of the days that had gone before made her even more uneasy. It seemed entirely too prophetic.

Gideon came back in a little over ten minutes later. He was dressed in khakis that molded the beautifully sculptured line of his thighs and a cream shirt with the sleeves rolled up to his elbow to bare his muscular forearms. His damp hair was combed with the unaccustomed meticulousness of a scrubbed and spiffy little boy, she noted, with a sudden rush of tenderness. But there was nothing boyish about Gideon's demeanor as he sat down opposite her at the table and began to eat. There was only quiet competence, maturity and a seriousness that worried her.

It wasn't until after they had finished the meal itself and were having coffee that Gideon leaned back and gazed somberly at her. "I want you to marry me."

Serena almost dropped her coffee cup. A swift surge of joy was followed by confusion and then an odd sense of panic. "You don't mean it."

"I mean it." Gideon's lips thinned to a tight line. "Did you think we could continue this little idyll forever? It's time we came out of the rosy haze and talked about commitment."

"Marriage," she echoed. Her throat felt dry and tight and she moistened her lips nervously.

"You seem to be having trouble with the idea. I don't know why. It's not such an unusual concept." He pushed his cup and saucer aside with barely controlled impatience. "Despite the liberated era we live in, it's still considered the thing to do when two people care for each other, you know." He paused before adding, "And you do care for me, Serena."

"Yes, of course I do." There was no question in her mind. How could anyone help loving Gideon? He was all sunlight and passion. He was quiet strength and laughter. "I think we ought to wait a while before we take such a serious step. We've really only known each other a little less than a week." Her smile was uncertain. "Why don't we talk about it again later?"

"Now. I want to talk now, Serena."

"Well, I don't." She pushed her chair back and stood up. "You're being unreasonable. There's no reason we can't go on exactly as we have been." She drew a deep shaky breath and smiled pleadingly. "Would it be so bad? You can't say you haven't enjoyed the last few days."

His expression lost none of its quiet determination. "No, I can't deny it. That's why it's important we keep what we have. Marriage, Serena." He rose to his feet and stood facing her across the table. "It's got to be marriage."

"Not yet," she said sharply. "I've been married, dammit. It would be foolish to jump impulsively into such a serious commitment." She smiled with an effort. "Now why don't we discuss something else? We obviously can't agree on the subject of marriage."

He shook his head. "Not this time, Serena. I've watched you sidestep any hint of commitment for the entire time we've been together." His lips curved wryly. "I don't think you were even conscious of doing it. Heaven knows our time together has been so damn wonderful I didn't want to blow it by pushing too hard, but we can't put it off any longer. Our time's running out." He gestured toward the door. "Come on, we're going to talk."

"The dishes—"

"We'll do them later," Gideon said firmly. He tossed his napkin on the table, turned and strode from the room.

She gazed mutinously after him before reluctantly following him down the hall and into the library. She seated herself stiffly in a flowered easy chair and folded her hands in her lap. "Perhaps you'd better begin the discussion," she said. "I've said everything I wish to on the subject."

He dropped down on the couch and regarded her sardonically. "Which is absolutely nothing. But I don't mind taking the initiative. Suppose we start by my asking a question or two." He leaned forward, his gaze fixed with hypnotic intensity on her face. "What happens after we leave here, Serena? My base is here and yours is in New York. What did you have in mind for our relationship then?"

"I'm sure we could work something out."

"I'm sure we could. Perhaps we could take turns commuting on weekends. And there's always the telephone, isn't there, Serena? I'm sure we'd find long-distance heavy breathing more than satisfying."

"Don't be sarcastic," Serena said. "It wouldn't have to be forever. Just until we feel sure what we're doing is right."

"I'm sure," he said between his teeth. "And you're sure too, dammit!" He made an effort at control. "Look, I know you're afraid, but I—"

"I'm not afraid. I just think—"

"The hell you're not!" His dark eyes were blazing. "Do you think I don't know you love me? That's the one thing in the world I'm damn certain about. There's no way that what we've got together could be one-sided. You're just so scared you're shaking in your shoes."

"That's ridiculous. Why should I be afraid?"

"You shouldn't be afraid, but you are. There's nothing to fear in what we have together. I know whatever you're afraid of has something to do with what happened to you that night, or in the years we were separated, and I know your marriage wasn't what a marriage should be, but ours would be different. We can straighten everything out if you'll only let me help you. But I can't help you, if you won't talk about it. *Talk* to me."

She stared dumbly at him.

"Dammit, don't look at me like that." He stood up with the leashed ferocity of a caged leopard. "You've been a fantastic lover, but I need more than sex. I need you to trust me and let me become a part of you. Sex isn't enough and I won't let you use it as a substitute." He turned to the door. "And I damn well can't take it any longer!"

"Where are you going?" she asked, startled.

"For a walk."

"But it's pouring rain!"

"Good." He cast her a glance as tempestuous as the storm outside. "Maybe it will cool me off." He strode out of the room and a moment later she heard the front door slam behind him.

She was stunned and bewildered. Gideon had been angry with her. Her own defensive anger had disappeared, submerged in the sudden panic that realization brought. He had always been so patient, so infinitely gentle with her, and now he was furious. What if he decided to leave her?

She jumped to her feet and ran from the room. A moment later she was down the porch steps and out into the darkness. "Gideon," she called frantically. "Come back!"

Which way had he gone? She couldn't see anything through the pelting rain. She was soaked to the skin, and the water was dripping from her throat down the low neckline of the caftan. She started running. "Gideon, where are you? I can't see—" She broke off as she collided with something blessedly familiar. Her arms went around him and she held him tight. "Gideon."

"You didn't have to come after me. I was coming back." She could sense the crooked smile on his lips. "I decided sex wasn't such a bad substitute after all. For now."

She clung harder to him. "I'm trying. I *am* trying, Gideon. But it's as if there's a wall I can't seem to climb over, or a river without a bridge. Please believe me, I'm trying to give you everything you want."

His lips brushed her forehead. "I know you're trying. I shouldn't have blown up, but sometimes I get so damn impatient." He paused. "And scared."

Her head lifted and her gaze searched his face in the darkness. "Scared?"

"I guess I wasn't really fair to you in there. You're not the only one who gets frightened. I'm scared I won't be enough for you. That was why I didn't come to you right away when those detectives found you. When the report came in, I found out you had jet-setter parents, and had attended fancy schools and even married a damn prince. And I was a cowboy from Texas without even a high-school education. I'd always tried to read and learn as much as possible, but I knew it wasn't the same. So I had to try to cram a four-year college education into as little time as possible."

"What!"

"Oh, I know I didn't get the same kind of polish as the people you must have known but—"

"Gideon, shut up." She couldn't tell if the moisture on her face was rain or tears. "My God, you're the best human being I've ever met and you're worried about *polish*? You're tender and warm and intelligent and—" She stopped, searching for words. "Everything. You don't need anything more than you have right now."

"Yes, I do," he said quietly. "I need you." He suddenly chuckled. "And I'll get you, too, just wait and see." He turned, his arm around her waist, urging her in the direction of the porch. "Come on, let's get back to the house before we drown out here. Then we'll hop into a hot shower together and I'll show you just how much I need you. You know, it's going to be kind of nice lying in bed together with the rain pounding on the roof. We haven't done that since the first night I met you. When I was a kid I used to love to hear the sound of the rain and think how green it was going to make the earth and how beautiful the flowers would be. . . ."

Five

Serena turned the bacon, experiencing a good deal of difficulty working around Gideon's arms, which were holding her in an affectionate hug. He seemed to have a fondness for attacks from the rear, she thought with amusement. His cheek brushed aside her ponytail as his lips started to nuzzle the nape of her neck. "Gideon, you're supposed to be making toast."

"I am making toast." His hands slipped beneath the loose cream shirt she was wearing to rub her midriff with lazy sensuous strokes. "The toaster is automatic." His hands roved up to cup her bare breasts in his palms and began to squeeze their fullness while his thumbs flicked at her nipples teasingly.

She caught her breath, as she felt her breasts tauten and swell in his hands. "Well, this frying pan isn't," she said thickly. "I'm going to burn the bacon."

"That's simple enough." He pressed closer so she could feel his rock-hard arousal against her bottom. "Turn it off."

His fingers were plucking at her nipples and she was beginning to see everything through a heated haze. She heard a mechanical ping somewhere across the room. "The toast is up," she said vaguely.

"That's not all." Gideon voice was ragged. "I never knew making breakfast could be such a turn-on. Of course, your running around in just my shirt could have something to do with it."

"I have a pair of shorts on," she protested, then tensed as his hand dove down between her thighs and squeezed teasingly.

"So you have. What a disappointment." One hand was rubbing her with a slow circular motion that caused her to arch back against him convulsively, while the other left her breast to pick up the frying pan and put it on the back burner. "The bacon's burning, Serena." His lips nibbled at her ear before nipping sharply. "And so are we. Don't you think we should do something about it?"

"Maybe we'd better," she said breathlessly. "It's obvious we're not going to eat breakfast until we satisfy a few other appetites."

He chuckled. "I knew you were a clear-thinking woman." He drew her back from the stove and with his arm around her waist, he led her to a straight-backed kitchen chair and pulled her onto his lap. "You're absolutely right." He stared to unbutton her shirt.

Her eyes widened. "Here?"

"Why not? It's closer than the bedroom." He whirled her around until she was astraddle him. The bold shock of his manhood pressed against her, separated by only a few layers of material, and sent a hot liquid melting to her loins. He had the shirt unbuttoned now and was impatiently pushing it aside. "Wouldn't you find it erotic to make love in the kitchen?" He was punctuating his words with tiny teasing strokes with his tongue at her nipples. "I'd like to make love to you on every piece of furniture in the whole damn house." He blew teasingly at one taut peak. "Then, no matter where I was, I could look around and think about what you said, and what you did." He smiled as she gave a little half gasp as his teeth nipped at her nipple. "How you wanted me in just that particular spot." Two fingers slid beneath the cuff of her shorts and began stroking her with a rhythm that caused her to clench around those skillful intruders as if to hold them captive within her. "And you do want it right now, right here, don't you, love?"

A shudder shook her as her hands clenched on his shoulders in a spasm of need. "Yes," she gasped. "Right here, right now."

"And so do I." He fumbled at the snap of his jeans. "Help me. I don't want to leave you."

Her trembling hands slid down to the zipper and they were even clumsier than his at the task.

"What the hell!"

Serena looked up, startled at the violent imprecation. Then she, too, heard the strident knocking that had failed to pierce the passionate haze surrounding their senses. Knocking? There hadn't been any visitors in all the time they'd been here. "Who'd come calling here?"

"At the moment, I don't give a damn, as long as they go away." The pounding intensified, becoming heavier and more demanding. "Which our visitor evidently doesn't intend to do. Damn, what lousy timing. Button up, Serena." He tweaked a nipple affectionately. "But be sure to remember where we were." He lifted her off his lap, stood up and strode swiftly out of the kitchen.

Serena automatically began buttoning the shirt as she followed him slowly into the hall. Like Gideon, she was experiencing intense frustration and annoyance, but it was also mixed with curiosity. Gideon had arranged for them to be so totally isolated here on the plantation that it had seemed like another planet. Now, abruptly, their isolation had been disturbed and she wanted to see who dared to intrude.

Gideon was frowning impatiently as he threw open the door. "What the hell are you doing here?"

"At the moment I'm nursing some very bruised knuckles from pounding on this door for the last five minutes," Ross drawled. "May I come in?"

Gideon reluctantly stepped aside. "Why the devil are you here, Ross? I told you we'd contact you when we were ready to come back to Mariba."

"It was a matter that couldn't wait and I didn't think you'd want anyone at the hotel relaying this particular message." His gaze drifted over Gideon's shoulder to where Serena was standing in the shadows at the end of the hall. "Hello, Serena, I'm glad you're here. This concerns you too."

"What do you mean?" She came forward to stand

beside Gideon. She suddenly felt an icy ripple of dread go through her. "Dane?"

Ross nodded grimly. "They wouldn't let me see him last night, and Mendino sent a message to Gideon."

Gideon froze, his body radiating tension. "What message?"

"He'll release Dane into your custody for the sum of five hundred thousand dollars cash." Ross paused. "Or he'll send him to the Devil's Plate."

"Devil's Plate?" Serena asked.

"It's one of the more hellish prisons on Castellano." Gideon explained, not looking at her. "How does he think he can get away with this? I'll wring the little son of a bitch's neck."

"He's scared," Ross said. "The people have been rioting in the streets for the last three days and the junta may be overthrown at any time. My guess is Mendino wants escape money. Anyone high up in the military will receive an automatic death sentence once the revolutionary forces take power. At the moment, he's more afraid of them than he is of you."

Gideon began to swear beneath his breath. "It wasn't supposed to be this soon. Julio told me—" He broke off. "What are the chances of Mendino giving us Dane if we pay the ransom?"

Ross shrugged. "Not good. He's a greedy bastard and crooked as they come. He'll probably take Dane with him and try to gouge Serena or the kid's parents."

"I've got to go back to Mariba right away," Serena said. "There's got to be something we can do. I have some money—"

"If it were merely a question of money, don't you think I'd give it to the bastard?" Gideon asked harshly. "It's *my* fault Dane is being used as a pawn. I set him up."

"And I let him stay there, instead of fighting you," Serena said wearily. "I thought he'd be safe."

"Only because I told you he'd be safe." Gideon was pale beneath his tan. "As God is my witness, I didn't have the slightest doubt he'd be perfectly secure, Serena. I knew this uprising was coming, but I was told by someone I trust that things wouldn't come to a boil until at least a month from now."

"What's the use of arguing about who's to blame," Serena cried frantically. "We've got to get him out of there right *now.*"

"We will." Gideon spoke with total certainty. "I'll get him out. I promise you, Serena, he'll be out by tomorrow night." He turned to face Ross. "Go back to Mendino and tell him we'll give him the money. Try to stall him as long as you can about the delivery time. Tell him it will take time to arrange for that much cash."

Serena turned toward the stairs. "Wait for me, Ross. I'm going with you."

"No," Gideon said sharply. "Mariba isn't safe for you. What's to stop Mendino from taking you hostage too? Besides, there's nothing you could do there. Mendino won't let anyone see Dane."

She wheeled and strode back to him. "I've got to *do* something. I can't just sit here and wait."

"You will be doing something. We can do more here right now than in Mariba."

"How? Dane's in Mariba, dammit."

"Easy." Gideon's tone was soothing. "I know you're upset and worried nearly crazy, but trust me. You heard what Ross said; you know that money alone won't do the trick. We'll have to find another way."

"What other way?"

"We'll have to work through the revolutionaries."

"But they're in *Mariba*." Serena twisted her fingers through her ponytail. "Are you trying to drive me crazy?"

"Not all of them are on Castellano," Gideon said. "One of the principal ringleaders is here on Santa Isabella. We'll contact him tonight and make arrangements for Dane's rescue."

"Oh, Lord, it all sounds so dangerous," Serena whispered. "Revolutions, and juntas, and nightmare prisons."

"I know." Gideon's hands closed on her shoulders. "I can't promise you there won't be danger, but I won't let Dane be hurt."

"How can you stop it?"

He tried to smile. "I'm a steamroller, remember? I'll roll right over them." He lifted her chin. "For heaven's sake, don't cry. I don't think I could take it."

"He's only twenty-one years old." Serena's voice was shaking. "I've always tried to take care of him. I'm so scared I've failed him this time."

"You haven't failed anyone. All this is my fault, not yours." Gideon's lips tightened. "And I'll be the one to set it right." His hands dropped away from her and he took a step back. "Run along and pack a change of clothes. You'll need jeans, tennis shoes, and a light jacket. We'll want to be ready to go right after we contact Julio."

"Who is Julio?"

"That's an interesting question," Ross said dryly. "Julio Rodriguez is something of an enigma. I'm not sure anyone knows who or what he is, but he's definitely interesting."

"He's the revolutionary leader?" Serena asked.

Gideon nodded. "In a manner of speaking. Julio's position is a little complicated. I'll send word to him to meet us at my hotel on the other side of the island. Julio prefers crowds."

"Will he help us?"

"He damn well better. He was the one who told me Dane would be safe for the next month." Gideon smiled grimly. "Oh, yes, he'll help us. We'll have dinner in the hotel dining room and then go to the nightclub afterward. He'll be at either one or the other." His gaze searched her face. "Will you be all right alone? I'm going to have Ross drop me at the hotel so that I can set up the meeting with Julio."

"I'll be fine. I'll do your packing too." Lord knew she needed something to do to keep her mind off Dane's dangerous situation. "Is there any other way I can help?"

He shook his head. "I'll be back in a few hours and pick you up to take you to the hotel. Try to take a nap. I don't know how much rest we'll get once we contact Julio."

"How do you expect me to—" She broke off. Even to her own ears her voice had sounded half hysterical. She mustn't fall apart. Gideon was right. There was no telling how far their resources would be stretched before this was over. "I'll try. Good-bye, Gideon." She started up the stairs.

Gideon stood at the foot of the stairs and watched her until she disappeared from view.

"She took it very well," Ross said soberly. "Damn, I hated to bring her news like that."

"Why? None of it was your responsibility. I'm the one who gave the orders and made the decisions. I'm the one she's going to hate, if anything happens to him." His skin was drawn tightly over his cheekbones and the expression in his eyes was sick. "But no more than I'll hate myself." He turned to the door. "Come on, let's get moving. There's no way I'm going to let Mendino do this."

"*That's* your hunted revolutionary, skulking among the shadows?" Serena shook her head in bewilderment as she tried to catch another glimpse of Julio Rodriguez among the crowd on the dance floor. "Is this some kind of joke?"

"Julio is no joke—just a bit unusual." Gideon took a sip of his bourbon. "He's definitely a free spirit in more ways than one. As for being hunted, the *guardia* of Castellano has agents who would be overjoyed to assassinate him, but as long as he doesn't allow himself to be caught off guard, he's safe enough on Santa Isabella. He's one of the island's wealthiest citizens and owns a private air charter service and several coffee plantations here."

"If all his property and interests are here, why is he trying to overthrow the government of Castellano?"

"His old friend, Consuela Jiménez, was raped and murdered by the *guardia* two years ago,"

Gideon said grimly. "Since then, he's supplied money, arms, and transportation to the rebels on a regular basis. He may be a little unconventional, but if anyone can arrange to get Dane out of Mariba, it will be Julio."

"Dear heaven, I hope so," she whispered. Then misgivings bombarded her again as the crowd parted and she caught another glimpse of Julio Rodriguez. She didn't know how she could have lost sight of him even for a moment. He was almost six feet five and his apparel stood out like a neon sign among the dark tuxedos of the other men on the dance floor. He wore scarlet trousers that hugged his buttocks and thighs with loving detail and a white silk shirt unbuttoned almost to his waist. The gold chain encircling his tan throat glittered as he undulated opposite an elegantly gowned blond. He was shockingly different from the sleek, expensively dressed patrons of the nightclub. "I gather you don't have a dress code here."

"Julio has an exemption," Gideon said. "He can be very persuasive."

Serena could believe it. The blond with whom he danced was looking up at him as if she were starving, and he was prime rib with all the trimmings. There was no question that Julio Rodriguez was very attractive. He was very Latin, and darkly handsome. His flashing white smile managed to be sensual and endearing at the same time. "Let's hope that he puts his persuasion to good use with Mendino."

"I don't think persuasion will be the order of the day," Gideon said as he caught Julio's eye and motioned to him. "He's seen us; he should be right over."

Serena saw Julio bow elegantly to the disappointed blond, smile with enough wattage to light up New York City, and then start to make his way through the crowd. He walked as gracefully as he danced, and as he drew closer she realized he was probably older than she had first thought, perhaps in his late twenties. She found she was becoming accustomed to his outrageous garb and it no longer jarred her. Somehow that color and dash belonged to Julio Rodriguez, as the traditional "suit of lights" belonged to a matador.

Gideon rose to his feet and shook hands with Rodriguez and then turned to Serena. "Julio Rodriguez, Serena Spaulding. Now that we have the formalities out of the way, sit down and tell me what the hell went wrong. You said—"

Julio held up his hand as he dropped into the chair opposite Serena. "I know, I know. It was as much a surprise to me as it was to you." His expression was somber as he gazed at Serena. "I'm very sorry. It was my fault that Gideon blundered so badly. His plan to win you appealed to my romantic side, and I truly thought I was giving him the right information. Unfortunately, sometimes events occur that change our plans."

Gideon sat down again. "And what 'event' occurred this time?"

"'The *guardia* executed the editor of the largest newspaper in Mariba four days ago,' Julio said simply. "The rioting was completely spontaneous, but we're going to take advantage of popular opinion to strike while the iron is hot."

"Not before I get Dane out of Mariba." Gideon's expression was flint hard. "The junta could initiate a bloodbath, if they think their regime is on the verge of toppling."

Serena felt the panic rise within her. "When is all this supposed to happen?"

Julio's eyes glowed with gentle sympathy. "I'm sorry, I can't tell you that, but it's best we move quickly."

"We?" Gideon asked. "You're going with us?"

Julio looked at Gideon in surprise. "Of course. I share the blame, so it follows that I should also share the danger." His grin flashed bold and brilliant in his dark face. "Besides, when the real action starts it will be a group effort, and I've always worked better alone. This exercise will be a nice little warm-up."

"Castellano will be dangerous for you," Gideon said slowly. "The *guardia* have your name and picture."

Julio shrugged. "So? I know Castellano like the back of my hand, and I have friends everywhere."

"Some in very high places." Gideon took a sip of his drink. "One of them paid me a visit the day before I left Mariba. Alessandra sends her regards."

Julio smiled. "Oh, she contacted you? I gave her your name and she thinks you would be an excellent distributor. She thought I was a little too close to the revolutionary forces to trust with it. Did you come to an agreement?"

Gideon nodded. "I accepted her offer. How could I refuse?"

Julio's expression softened. "You couldn't, my friend. Not in a million years. That's why I sent her to you." He pushed back his chair and stood up. "I'll meet you at the airport in an hour. Miss Spaulding is going with us?"

"Yes, of course," Serena said quickly.

A faint smile tugged at Julio's lips. "There's no 'of course' about it. Not many women would want to plunge into a revolution on an island like Castellano. Remind me to introduce you to my old friend Kate Lantry sometime. I think you'd have a great deal in common." He bowed and gave her the same blindingly sensual smile he had given the blond on the dance floor. Serena had a shrewd idea that sensuality came as naturally as breathing to him, for when he spoke, his tone was casually platonic. "You're both lovely and have a habit of going after what you want. It will be like old times."

Then he was gone, skirting both the dance floor and the blond as he made his way to the entrance of the club.

"You're right. He's very unusual," Serena said with a thoughtful frown as she gazed after Rodriguez. "But I think I like him."

"Most women do," Gideon said dryly. "Most men, too, for that matter. Probably the reason he's one of my best friends is that when Julio's around, I'm never bored. Are you ready to leave?"

"In a minute." Her gaze lowered to rest on the glass of wine in front of her. "Who is Alessandra?" She could feel his gaze on her face, but she refused to look up. "Or isn't it any of my business?"

"I don't have any business that's not your business," Gideon said softly. "We were talking about Alessandra Karpathan. Perhaps you've heard of her.

Heaven knows her wedding to Sandor Karpathan and his election to the presidency of Tamrovia were all over the papers a year ago."

Her glance lifted to his in surprise. "I remember seeing something about it at the time. What was she doing in Castellano?"

"It seems that the lady has a pet charity project. She visits oppressed and war-torn countries and sets up a distribution chain of money and food to needy children. She usually chooses someone with contacts, but no close political affiliations, to carry out the distribution." His lips twisted wryly. "I was perfectly willing to go along with her plans, but she picked a damnably inconvenient time to make her appearance. I could hardly wait to get rid of her the afternoon you arrived."

Serena felt a rush of relief as she realized the woman Gideon had escorted to her limousine that afternoon was not a lover, but a partner in a charitable enterprise. She hadn't admitted even to herself until this moment how the shadowy memory of the magnificently sensual woman had bothered her. "I think I caught sight of her for a moment on the patio. She's very attractive."

"Yes, and she has a mind like a steel trap." Gideon's tone was abstracted as he stood up. "I think we'd better leave now. I have a few arrangements to make with Ross by phone before we meet Julio."

Serena quickly rose. "I'll go change and meet you in the lobby in fifteen minutes."

Gideon nodded. "Fine. I'll change after I make my call and see about finding a gun. I haven't needed one since the early days on Castellano."

"You don't have to get one for me. I brought a thirty-two revolver with me. I packed it in a suitcase I checked through. The customs officer in Castellano just waved me through."

He looked a little startled. "Do you always take a gun with you when you travel?"

"Rarely. These circumstances were a bit different," she said calmly. "But I always keep one at the cottage and you'll find I'm moderately competent. I've been a woman on my own for a good many years. It was only sensible to learn how to protect myself."

Gideon took her elbow and began to propel her across the dance floor toward the entrance. "Very sensible."

"Then why were you so shocked?"

"I guess I'm not so much shocked as uneasy," he said thoughtfully. "It reminded me how much we still have to learn about each other. I seem to have known you forever, yet we've only just scratched the surface." His clasp tightened on her arm. "Well, I imagine we'll find out a hell of a lot more about each other once we get back to Castellano. A situation like this one has a way of stripping us bare of all our protective barriers. And maybe that won't be such a bad thing."

Six

"What in heaven's name is wrong, Gideon?" Serena asked. She had been conscious of the tension radiating from Gideon ever since they had landed in a tiny glade in the middle of the rain forest. At first, she had paid little attention to it; she had been pretty tense herself, and the heavy blackness of the junglelike forest hadn't helped to alleviate it. But the emotion gripping Gideon was somehow ... different, and seemed to be increasing every second as they followed Julio through the tropical foliage.

"Nothing." Gideon's voice was hoarse, oddly tight. "I just don't happen to care for this kind of terrain. It brings back too many memories of Nam." He drew a deep, shuddering breath. "I can't *breathe* here. Where the hell is Julio going?"

The air was unquestionably hot and humid, but Serena was having no trouble breathing. She slipped her hand into Gideon's in silent support.

"Who knows? But I'm willing to follow him nearly anywhere after that landing. I was sure he was going to crack up. That field was hardly larger than a postage stamp."

Gideon nodded. "He's a fantastic pilot. Let's hope he's an equally fantastic guide. We don't have time to get lost in this damn forest."

"You malign me," Julio said reproachfully. He was leaning against the bole of a huge rain tree a few yards ahead of them. He flicked the beam of his flashlight up to see their faces. "You should know by now that I'm fantastic at anything I turn my hand to, Gideon. I know exactly where we are."

"Good, then you can tell me when we're going to get out of this damn rain forest," Gideon said.

The smile left Julio's face. "I'm sorry, Gideon, I forgot about Na Peng. This forest was the safest place for the two of you to wait, until I could contact Ross. Shall we scratch it, and go on to the fishing village instead?"

"No." Gideon's hand unconsciously tightened on Serena's. "That would be criminally self-indulgent of me. Just get us out of here as soon as you can."

"I will. Wait here." Julio disappeared behind a bank of thick shrubbery and immediately emerged with a ladder. He set it against the rain tree and turned to face them. "Climb up and make yourself comfortable. I'll go on to the village and meet with Ross. I should be back in a few hours."

"Make ourselves comfortable in a *tree*?" Serena asked blankly.

Julio chuckled. "I forgot to tell you there was a tree house behind those overhanging branches.

Kate and I built it when we first came to Castellano. I assure you it's quite habitable. Kate even lived there for a while. For the past two years we've been using it as a refuge for political prisoners we managed to rescue from the hands of the junta. Sometimes it was days before it was safe to land a plane and get them off the island." He turned away. "Be sure you close the shades before you light the lamp. The foliage of the rain tree is fairly dense, but you don't want to take the chance of being seen." The last words were barely audible as Julio faded into the forest. Dressed in dark jeans and a black flight jacket, he immediately became one with the shadows. Serena would never have believed that the colorful Julio she had first seen at the hotel could be so quickly transformed into the competent, businesslike pilot who had met them at the airport on Santa Isabella only a few hours earlier. Ross was right. The man was an enigma.

She turned back to face the ladder propped against the tree. "Well, I've always wanted to have a tree house. Let's see if Julio's fulfills all our childhood fantasies."

Gideon didn't answer and she cast him an anxious glance as she began to climb the ladder. The force field of tension surrounding him had taken on added dimension, and his palm had felt cold and clammy before she had released it to grasp the rungs of the ladder.

Serena stepped from the ladder onto a platform, and crossed the few feet to the tree house. The door swung open on well-oiled hinges and she peered inside. Though the room was small, the

ceiling was high enough for a tall man to stand
upright. The beam of Serena's flashlight skimmed
quickly around the room. The furnishings were
very simple. Mattresses, one pushed against the
far wall and the other beneath the window by the
door, a rattan chest on which a hurricane lamp
had been placed, and a nightstand on the far side
of the room beside the mattress. Touching at-
tempts at decoration appeared here and there,
There was a polished black vase on the nightstand, and another tall vase occupied a corner.
Both vases were empty, as were the rattan holders
affixed to the unfinished walls. The denim covers
on the mattresses appeared to be pristine, and an
air of warm coziness pervaded the tiny room.
Strange, considering the sparseness of furniture.
It should have appeared stark and bare, but this
was not the case. She felt as if all it would take
would be a little care, and this small haven would
come to life. Something warm and loving lingered
here. "I like it." The cone of light played on the
woven hemp shutters at the large window next to
the door. "I guess I should leave the shutters closed,
if we're going to light the lamp."

"No!" Gideon's voice was sharp. "We don't need
the lamp. There's no air in here." He strode past
her into the room and threw open the shutters.
"Turn off the flashlight. There's enough moonlight filtering through the branches to see our
way around the room." He stood there a minute
at the window and inhaled several times, as if his
lungs were starved for oxygen. Then he sat down
on the mattress closest to the window, drawing

up his knees and wrapping his arms around them.
"Come and sit down."

Gideon was correct. The moonlight was bright
enough to reveal all Serena wanted to see and a
few things that she didn't. Gideon's skin was
stretched tight over his cheekbones and his lips
were a flat line. "Would you like me to leave
then?" she asked gently.

He was silent for a moment, as if he were un-
dergoing a struggle. "If you wouldn't mind." There
was a thread of desperation in his laughter.
"I'm sorry. I know I'm being stupid."

She crossed the distance separating them
and dropped down on the mattress beside him.
His arm immediately went around her and she
cuddled closer. "You're not being stupid at all. It's
very close in here. This is much nicer."

"Yes." His chest was lifting and falling with the
harshness of his breathing.

"Would it help to talk about it?" she asked quietly. "Na Peng, I mean."

"Maybe. I don't know." His voice was unutterably weary. "I'll have to tell you sometime. It's part
of me, and it's not fair to shut you out."

"I don't want you to tell me if it's going to be
difficult for you."

"Easy or difficult, it doesn't matter. You have the
right." He closed his eyes, his breathing was shallow. "Na Peng was a prison camp. I was captured
and held there for five months. It was . . . hid-
eous. The atrocities were unbelievable, not only
on the military prisoners but on the Vietnamese
civilians." He took a breath and hurried on as if he
wanted to get it out. "There was a little Vietnamese

girl . . . she couldn't have been more than four-teen. I don't know what she was supposed to have done, but they made us come out into the middle of the compound and watch her punishment. They killed her infant son before her eyes and then took turns raping her." His voice lowered to a tone scarcely audible. "She died the next day."

"My God," Serena whispered. She felt sick. Her arms slid around his waist and held him close.

"I escaped the next month, but I didn't f way back to our lines for another th He tried to smile. "And now you know wh particularly like rain forests."

But he hadn't accepted Julio's alternate when it had been offered, Serena thought, and had probably been because of her that he had refused. "Gideon—" Her voice broke. "Why the hell didn't we go with Julio?"

"No, it's okay. We have to fight these bush-whackers, remember? If we let them beat us, they hold on forever and we're never safe." He opened his eyes and she could see the moisture as it beaded on his forehead and then rolled down his face. "Just hold me, please?"

"Yes." She was aching, bleeding inside. Julio, dammit, get *back* here, she thought desperately. "I'm not going anywhere."

"It's all around us. That's what's so bad. Even with my eyes closed, I can hear the night sounds and see . . ."

They stayed like that for an eternity, holding each other. At least, it seemed like an eternity to Serena. Gideon spoke in fragments, but those fragments drew vivid and heart-wrenching pic-

tures and finally he didn't speak at all. He just sat there and held her as if she were a life preserver thrown out onto a stormy sea.

"It's me." Julio's voice was blessedly cheerful as he called up to them from the ground. "I didn't think I'd risk getting a karate chop when I walked into the house, in case you thought it was the *guardia* that had stumbled on you."

Serena breathed a sigh of relief. Oh, thank heaven, now Gideon could get out of here.

Gideon's arms loosened and then dropped away from her. "I'm sorry," he whispered. "I didn't mean to be a burden to you."

She kissed him quickly, passionately. "Now you *are* being stupid."

"I seem to be constantly requiring comfort," he said with a crooked smile. "It's a good thing I don't have a particularly macho image of myself, or I'd be having serious ego problems at the moment."

"I've always hated that macho nonsense," Serena said. "And comfort should always go two ways."

"I think so too." There was a hint of sadness in his smile. "I think everything should be shared."

It was clear his words pertained to more than the present situation. She frowned in concern. "Gideon, I know—"

"Why are you sitting in the dark?" Julio stood in the doorway, the beam of his flashlight spotlighting the two of them. "It's time to get moving, Gideon. I brought Ross with me. He's waiting down below."

Serena scrambled to her feet. "Let's go."

Julio glanced at Gideon. "According to what Ross told me, I don't think you and I are included in Gideon's initial plan."

"Why not?" Serena's gaze went to Gideon.

Gideon stood up. "Ross and I have to do some preliminary wrangling with Mendino over the ransom." He didn't look at her. "We don't want the good colonel to become upset, do we? Once we have the situation set up, Julio can storm in for the big rescue." He grinned. "Julio's very good at flamboyant gestures."

"I want to go with you," Serena insisted.

Gideon shook his head. "Your presence would only complicate things. This little transaction won't take long. With any luck, it should be over by dawn. Julio will stay here with you until then."

"You're sure this is how you want to play it?" Julio asked gravely.

"I'm sure." Gideon turned to Serena and kissed her lingeringly. "Don't let this shameless philanderer seduce you. He's not safe when a woman and a mattress are in the same room."

Julio chuckled. "You insult me. Who needs a mattress? Don't worry, I'll take care of her, Gideon."

"I know you will." Gideon gave her another quick kiss. "Good-bye, love."

She opened her lips to protest again, but he was gone. She stared into space. There was something wrong, something about the way . . .

"It will be all right," Julio said comfortingly. "Gideon can take care of himself."

Her gaze flew to his face. "Why should he have to take care of himself? He said this was merely a negotiation."

"You're jumping at shadows." Julio moved to the window and closed the shutters. "It will be over soon. All we have to do is keep ourselves amused for a few hours." His white teeth gleamed as he smiled. "And, since Gideon is my friend, it eliminates the most obvious and pleasurable pastime." He crossed the room to the rattan chest, lit the hurricane lamp, and then turned off his flashlight. He held the lamp out to her. "Hold this, will you? There's a pack of cards in the chest." He lifted the lid and glanced back over his shoulder. "We'll play poker and get to know each other. Alas, not in the biblical sense." He chuckled. "And perhaps I'll tell you all about the woman who lived in this little house."

"*You* climb the damn tree. I'm going back to Mariba!"

It was Dane's voice!

Serena tossed the cards she had been shuffling onto the mattress and jumped to her feet. "He got him out! It's Dane, Julio! Gideon managed to get him released. I can't believe it." She tore across the room and flung open the door. "Isn't this wonderful?"

Julio hesitated. "Wonderful."

Serena teetered on the edge of the platform, peering down into the darkness. "Dane, come up here! I want to *see* you."

There was a short silence then Dane said grudgingly, "Okay, I'm coming up."

Serena backed a few paces to make room on the platform. Then Dane's curly black head appeared in the pool of lamplight issuing from the tree house. Oh thank heavens, he was *all right!* His expression was a bit stormy, but he wasn't hurt or . . . She hurled herself into his arms and hugged him with all her strength. "Damn you, Dane, I hope this will teach you something. The next time someone offers you a bacchanalian revel, check for strings, you idiot."

"There weren't any strings," he protested. "And I had a helluva good time, until that ass Mendino turned into a minor Hitler." He gave her a quick hug and pushed her away. "Thanks for riding to the rescue anyway." He scowled. "And now that you've seen I'm all right, I'm going back to Mariba. I never would have left, if I'd known about the damned deal. I had my party and I'll pay the piper."

"What deal are you talking about?" Serena asked.

"I'm going back for Gideon Brandt," Dane growled. "What do you all think I am? An irresponsible kid? I told you, I had my fun and I'll be the one to pay for it."

Serena went still. "What do you mean, go back for Gideon?"

"Gideon stayed in Mariba," Ross said as he negotiated the last few rungs of the ladder and stepped onto the platform. "He made a deal with Mendino. He promised him another two hundred thousand in ransom, if he'd let Dane go and accept him as hostage instead."

She was terrified. "Why?" Her lips felt numb and her voice sounded wooden. "We were going to free Dane anyway. Julio was— "

"Gideon thought there was an element of risk involved." Ross was choosing his words carefully.

"He didn't believe that he had the right to take that risk since he felt responsible for Dane's predicament. He called me tonight from Santa Isabella and told me to set up the new deal with Mendino."

Dane muttered a low curse.

Serena ignored him, her gaze fastened on Ross's face. "What kind of risk?"

Ross shrugged. "I told you Mendino was unpredictable."

"But what does that *mean*?" Serena grated out between her teeth.

"It means he wasn't sure which way Mendino would jump when we launched the assault." It was Julio's quiet voice behind her. "He's very volatile and—"

"Julio," Ross said warningly.

"No." Julio moved to stand beside them on the platform. "She's a strong woman. Don't treat her as if she were a child. I don't think it was fair of Gideon not to tell her what he was planning to do. Women can be a hell of a lot stronger than men when they have to be." He turned to Serena. "He was afraid Mendino would fly into a rage and shoot Dane before we managed to disarm them."

Serena could feel the blood draining from her face. She had thought she couldn't be more frightened, but she was wrong. "Then the same thing will apply to Gideon, won't it? Gideon is in the same danger?"

Julio nodded. "Perhaps even greater danger. Mendino will feel Gideon has made a fool of him."

"Then let's pay the ransom. Let's give them anything they want."

"It's too late," Ross said. "Julio says the entire

town will be a madhouse within a few hours. The headquarters of the junta is going to be stormed and Mendino will know it's the end. We can't manage to raise that amount of cash before that happens, so we either move in and try to take Mendino now, or we wait and see. There's a small chance that Mendino will release Gideon when he makes a run for it."

"A small chance," Serena repeated, anger burning through the layers of ice surrounding her. She was suddenly freed from the bonds of horror and fear and was alive again. Alive and enraged. "We're not going to take *any* chances with Gideon's life. We're not going to sit around and wait. And we're sure as hell *not* going to let some crazy colonel call the shots." She shivered. Shots. She wished she hadn't used that phrase. It brought Gideon's danger too vividly to mind. She moistened her lips. "The problem is that Gideon will be unarmed and vulnerable right before you break into the suite. Is that right?"

Julio nodded. "That's the problem."

"Then you need someone there to furnish him with a weapon and support. Right?"

"Right."

"I'll go," Dane said. "I tried to tell you before that it was my place—"

"No." Serena met Julio's gaze. "I'll be the one to go."

"Hell, no," Ross said roughly. "Gideon would strangle me, if I sent you into Mariba."

"You don't have any choice. No one is *sending* me anywhere. You idiots *let* Gideon put his head on the chopping block, and I'll be damned if he's going to stay there." She turned to Ross. "You're so good at negotiating deals. Start negotiating a way to get me to Gideon." She turned to Julio. "You." One finger punched Julio's chest. "You said you'd managed prison escapes before. You must know all kinds of methods to smuggle weapons. Get to work on it."

A tiny smile tugged at Julio's lips. "Yes, ma'am."

"Serena, Mendino is no pussycat," Dane said hesitantly. "Why don't you calm down, and I'll—"

"I'm no pussycat either." Serena's eyes blazed at the three men. "Though I've been behaving like a veritable tabby lately. How the hell do you think I managed to raise you and keep us fed all these years, Dane?"

A hint of mischief appeared in Dane's violet eyes. "You were a hit woman for the Mafia?"

"No, but I would have done almost anything at one time to make sure we were both free and clear of your wonderful father. I would have washed dishes, or run a bulldozer or collected garbage. We all do what we have to do and try to hold onto as much integrity and happiness as we can. So don't talk to me about pussycats." Her gaze met her brother's unflinchingly. "And you're right, Dane. Some of the blame is on your shoulders. So you can damn well go with Julio and help get Gideon out of this mess." She stopped for breath. "Now all of you get to work. I want to be in Gideon's suite at the Hotel Cartagena in two hours. You figure out how to get me there, *with* a weapon." She stepped back and slammed the door, leaving the three stunned men on the platform.

How quixotic, how stupid of Gideon to put himself in this danger, she thought angrily. They could have found some way to lessen the risk to Dane without Gideon placing himself in the exact same situation. Yet it was exactly the kind of foolishness Gideon would be guilty of committing. She should have realized how a man who collected stray dogs and waifs, and gave himself with such total commitment to the helpless as Gideon did, would react when he had learned he had been responsible for Dane's tenuous position. The softhearted idiot was bound to rush in and . . .

She leaned back against the door, tears running helplessly down her cheeks. She had to hold onto anger. It was the only way she could keep going until she could be with Gideon again. She mustn't remember how he had trembled in her arms doing those last hours before he had left for Mariba or how bravely he had fought those memories. The horror of his experieces at Na Peng had made those in her own past dwindle by comparison. He deserved nothing but joy now. He had paid his dues. Yet he had gone rushing to Dane's rescue like a knight in full armor. But Gideon didn't have any armor, or weapons.

How she loved him. She hadn't even given him those words to take with him. She had been so turned inward, so locked into her own prison of memories that she had let him batter against the walls and never once let him enter. He had shared everything with her—his strength, his weakness, his love—and she had returned only a pale imitation. She had told him there was a wall she couldn't climb, a river with no bridge, but why hadn't she realized that she, herself, had built that wall? She could have spanned that river at any time, if she had only let herself think clearly. Now anger and terror had ripped aside all the self-delusions and there was nothing left but truth.

She wiped her eyes with the back of her hand. It was stupid to stand here weeping when there were things to be done and Gideon to be saved. She had to be strong now. There would be time enough for softness when Gideon was free. Toughen up, but keep the loving. Gideon's words came back to her with aching poignancy. They had become the creed he lived by. Well, she was strong enough to be tough when she was forced, and Lord knows, she was brimming, overflowing, with love for Gideon. She just hoped she'd be able to tell him so before—

She blocked the thought quickly. Nothing was going to happen to Gideon. She straightened and unconsciously squared her shoulders. The time for tears was past. It was time to shoot a few bushwhackers out of the saddle.

Seven

The lobby of the Hotel Cartagena looked exactly like that of any other upper-middle-class hotel. There was the usual wine-colored carpet, green plants hanging in strategic places, and bellhops bustling back and forth. Serena didn't know quite what she had expected, but it wasn't this atmosphere of total matter-of-factness. She supposed she had assumed it would be something of an armed camp, with machine guns mounted on the reception desk.

Ross's hand was grasping her elbow and his words were a *sotto voce* stream in her ear as they crossed the lobby toward the bank of brass-trimmed mahogany elevators. "Now don't be belligerent with them. I don't think Medino would risk hurting you, but he's—"

"Unpredictable," Serena finished for him. "I believe I'm sick and tired of hearing about that particular characteristic of Mendino's." They entered the elevator and Ross inserted a key and then punched the button for the Royal Suite, which evidently occupied the entire fifteenth floor. The heavy doors closed and the elevator began to move with snaillike slowness. "I'm not about to be belligerent."

A faint smile tugged at Ross's lips. "You save that for your friends?"

"I was upset," she said, and then admitted honestly, "and frightened."

Ross's smile widened as he nodded understandingly. "Just tone it down with Mendino." He hesitated and his gaze slid away from her face. "They'll search you. That's why we didn't dare arm Gideon. Hopefully, they won't be as thorough with you as as they were with him." He paused again. "There aren't any women among Mendino's guards here, and Mendino and his officers are pretty rough. You're not going to like it."

"I know, Julio told me." She moistened her lips with her tongue. "It would be pretty stupid of me to let modesty weigh against saving Gideon." Her hands tightened nervously on the bamboo handles of her striped purse. "Don't worry, I won't give them any trouble."

"I made a big fuss about the two of you being lovers and you insisting on being with him. Mendino was very pleased to get another hostage and made no objection to your being in the same suite with Gideon, but he has none of the so-called gentler feelings where women are concerned." He still wasn't looking at her. "In fact, there were rumors about the death of his mistress last year.

You'll probably receive the same treatment he decides to mete out to Gideon."

"I didn't expect anything else."

"Julio has filled you in on our plans?"

"Yes, the bare outline. He didn't have time to go into anything in depth." Damn, this elevator was slow.

"You know that I won't be able to stay with you? I'll have to leave as soon as I deliver you to Mendino."

"Yes, Ross, we've gone over all this. Why repeat it?"

"Because I don't like the idea of you putting yourself in this kind of danger," he said with a scowl. "And Gideon's going to like it even less. To tell you the truth, I'm nervous as hell."

She smiled shakily at him. "Me, too."

His face softened. "It wouldn't hurt to show them you're a little tense. They'll expect it."

The elevator had finally stopped and Serena stiffened in apprehension. "No problem. I don't think I could hide it if I tried."

The doors opened with a *whoosh*, and Serena's heart jerked crazily and then began to pound in double time. Soldiers, guns—this was the scene she had expected downstairs. The elevator opened directly into the huge sitting room of the suite and there were at least twenty soldiers there.

Coming toward them was a golden-complexioned man in a dark green colonel's uniform. He was thin-faced, his pencil mustache a neat line over slightly pouty lips. A beaming smile lit his face, revealing a space between his front teeth. "Ah, Miss Spaulding, welcome. I am Colonel Pedro

Mendino. We are always happy to assist in reuniting lovers." His glance slowly ran over her, starting at the tips of her white high-heeled sandals, traveling over her slender figure in the slim white skirt and emerald silk blouse and ending as he met her eyes. The smile deepened as he read the apprehension she was experiencing and could not hide. He waved a hand. "There is only one minor formality to be gotten out of the way. Come this way, if you please."

Serena took a deep breath and stepped out of the elevator."

Gideon sat bolt upright in the morocco leather chair as she walked into the suite. "Serena?" he whispered.

She dropped her purse on the floor and ran across the room toward him. Then she was in his arms, pressing quick, loving kisses on his cheeks and throat between words. "Are you all right? I was so worried. What a stupid thing to do."

Mendino chuckled benevolently as he watched them from the doorway. "Is this not a wonderful surprise, Texan? Not only do we supply you with all the comforts, but your woman to warm your bed." He bowed with a touch of mockery and his voice took on a taunting note. "And she is ravishing, every single inch of her. I should know, I supervised the search myself."

Gideon's eyes darkened stormily as he opened his lips to speak.

Serena quickly covered his mouth with her own in a long passionate kiss. She heard Mendino laugh again and then the sound of the door closing behind her and the key turning in the lock. She lifted her lips to breathe softly. "Don't be crazy. It wasn't fun, but it wasn't bad."

"I bet," Gideon muttered. "What the hell are you doing here?"

She glanced quickly around the suite. "Microphone?" she mouthed.

He shook his head. "This was the same suite Dane occupied, and that certainly wasn't considered a high security operation."

"Good." She kissed him again. "You're such an idiot. Why do you have to be so damn noble?"

He frowned. "Why are you here? I'm going to draw and quarter Ross."

"He thought you'd only strangle him," she murmured. "And it's not his fault, it's yours. Did you think I was going to sit with my hands folded waiting for you to be either released or delivered back in a plastic sack? No way." Her arms dropped from around him and she took a step back. "There's something you'd better learn right now, Gideon—whenever you put yourself in danger, I'm going to be right behind you. You're so big on this sharing business, well, make up your mind we're going to share the bad too."

A reluctant smile banished his frown. "I thought I was doing what was best."

"You didn't even talk to me about it." She held up her hand to stop him when he started to speak. "Oh, I know, it's the pot calling the kettle black, but I'm going to change all that as soon as we get out of here. We'll share everything." Her gaze met his and suddenly her eyes were glittering with tears. "I was so frightened. Don't you ever do that to me again."

"I wouldn't dare," he said gently. "You're evidently a rip-roaring lady when you're riled." One finger gently touched her cheek. "Now, I gather you risked coming here for some reason other than the fact that you couldn't live without me."

"You're joking, but it's true, you know," she whispered. "I don't think I could live without you now. You might remember that the next time you're tempted to pull a stupid stunt like this." She forced herself to look away from him. She wanted to keep on gazing at him, touching him, just to assure herself he was really all right and they were together again. "What time it it?"

He glanced at his watch. "Nine twenty-six."

"Oh, Lord, the attack is going to take place in four minutes. We have to hurry. That search took much longer than we expected."

"Just how long did it take?" There was the timbre of steel beneath the silkiness of Gideon's tone.

"It doesn't matter." She hurried across the room to the door. "It's over now."

"It matters."

Serena snatched up the striped purse she had dropped on the floor when she had run into Gideon's arms. "Gideon, there isn't time for your possessive instincts to come to the fore. I need your help." She came back toward him.

"Who else was there besides Mendino?"

'A captain and a lieutenant," she said without thinking, then she saw his expression. "Gideon!"

"Very well, we'll drop it now. I know who they

are." He smiled with cold ferocity. "I just didn't want to target the wrong men." He looked down at the purse in her hands. "I assume you're not looking for a compact to powder your nose. A weapon?" His eyes narrowed thoughtfully. "Intriguing. They must have searched your purse. It would be the obvious thing to do."

"They did." She pulled the two six-inch bamboo handles off the pouch bag and then tossed the purse aside. "These are hollow, see?" She showed him the hole through the center of each piece of bamboo. "It's a blowgun."

"And just what are we supposed to blow?" Gideon asked.

"Hold them for a minute." She thrust the blowguns into his hand and rapidly unfastened her white skirt. She pulled her skirt and the half-slip beneath it down a few inches. "The appendix scar. It's rather large, but Julio said if anyone questioned it, I was to complain about what a butcher of a surgeon I had." She inserted her thumbnail beneath the top edge of the five-inch white scar and gently worked the adhesive loose. "It looks exactly like an old scar, doesn't it? Julio is really very clever." She had freed enough of the adhesive to gain a hold and with one strong pull she ripped the false scar from her abdomen. Four slender, needle-like darts fell to the carpet.

Gideon laughed helplesly as he bent to pick up the darts. "Only Julio would think of something like this."

"Be careful. Each tip is coated with a sedative strong enough to knock out a grizzly bear." She pulled up her slip and skirt and fastened the button at the waistband. She took one of the blow-guns and two of the darts from him. "Have you ever used one of these before?"

"No, have you?" His lips twitched. "It wouldn't surprise me if you had. You seem to take blow-guns, crazy colonels, and revolutions with amazing composure."

"I've never used one before, but the principle seems simple enough." Her tone was casual as she put one of the darts into the blowgun. "I imagine we'll have to be fairly close, though, and perhaps— Why are you laughing?"

"Because you look so damn beautiful, and you're talking like a cross between Sheena of the Jungle and a female James Bond." His eyes were glowing with warmth. "And because I'm so damn happy you're mine. I'd sure as hell hate to go up against—" He broke off as there was a sudden shout from the other room. "Right on time. Julio is to be congratulated." Then the rat-a-tat of machine-gun fire caused him to go tense. "I think we'd better get into position. I believe we may have a visitor at any moment." He crossed to the door and stepped to the side so that he would be behind the door when it swung open. "Come over here. I don't want you in the line of fire when Mendino barrels into the room."

"In just a second. I have one more thing to do." She set the blowgun and darts on the table beside her and ran over to the window. She drew back the curtains and struggled to open the window. It wouldn't budge!

"That's not a way out. It's fifteen stories down to the street and there's no fire escape."

"But I *have* to open it. Julio told me to do it."

"Well, Julio is going to be disappointed." Gideon put a dart into his blowgun. "This is a recently built hotel and the windows aren't constructed to open. The curse of an air-conditioned society is that fresh air is considered obsolete."

"Oh, damn, why didn't one of us think of this." Serena stopped tugging and looked wildly about the room. The desk chair! She rushed to the Louis XV desk and dragged its bowlegged chair back to the window.

"What are you doing?"

"I told you. Julio said I was to open the window." She picked up the chair and swung it with all her strength against the glass. It shattered, spraying shards in a sparkling shower. "I'm opening the window."

"I see you are," he said dryly. "I wish I could get you to obey *my* orders with such enthusiasm. Now, will you come back over here behind the door?"

"As soon as I get rid of these pieces of glass." She was knocking the remaining slivers of glass out of the pane. "There, that should do it. It wasn't so difficult. I guess—"

A key was turning in the lock!

"Oh, Lord," she whispered, turning to face the door. "I guess he heard it."

"Of course, he heard," Gideon muttered. "It was louder than the damn machine-gun fire. Quick—drop to the floor."

There was no time. Mendino was standing in the doorway, his face flushed and very ugly. There was a pistol in his hand and it was pointed straight at her. The open door made a barrier between Gideon and the colonel. Move forward, she prayed silently to herself. But Mendino simply stood there, aiming at her. Oh dear, she had to do something.

"Don't just stand there," Serena cried frantically. "Can't you see? Gideon's going to fall. I tried to stop him, but he said it was our only chance. He was going to crawl along the ledge."

Mendino's expression was arrested and then confused as his gaze went to the broken window. He took two steps into the room. It wasn't enough, but one more step would do it.

Serena kept her gaze from straying toward Gideon. It wasn't terribly difficult. Mendino's pistol seemed to fill her entire field of vision. "It's so far down there. I'm afraid he might slip and—"

Mendino took another step forward.

There was a low, whistling noise and Mendino's eyes widened and then glazed over as a tiny silver needle embedded itself in his neck. He fell to the floor, unconscious.

Gideon stepped from behind the door. "Serena, I think I may break your neck," he said grimly. "Why the hell didn't you do what I told you? What if Mendino had remembered that there wasn't a ledge?"

"Isn't there? That was all I could think of on the spur of the moment. And Julio told me to—"

"Serena, this is too much." Dane stuck his head through the opening she'd provided in the window, his eyes dancing. "When you ordered me to help Julio, you didn't tell me I'd have to do windows. I don't mind vacuuming or a little dusting, but I *never* do windows."

"The hell you don't." It was Julio's voice from somewhere beyond the window, but he was outside Serena's line of vision. "Will you stop chatting and get them out here? The diversion Ross and my men are providing can't cover us much longer. We were only able to smuggle four men up on the service elevator. Besides, I'm getting a nosebleed out here."

Serena took a step closer to the window. A window washer's scaffold was hanging suspended by two slender metal cords like a fragile gondola over the street far below. Dane and Julio stood on the platform gazing at her with remarkably similar expressions—mischief, excitement, and tremendous *joie de vivre.* "Now I know why you told me to open the window, but you never mentioned what a challenge it would be."

Julio grinned sheepishly. "How was I to know? I'm just a naive plantation owner, a regular old country boy. Where I come from, windows open."

"This one opened too." Serena found herself smiling back at him. "With a little persuasion." She glanced over her shoulder at Gideon. "Julio and Dane are going to take us for a little ride."

Gideon threw down the blowgun and picked up the gun Mendino had dropped. "Get on the scaffold. I'll be right back." He turned toward the door. "I have a little unfinished business."

"Gideon!" Serena's protest was almost a scream, but he was gone. "Oh, damn, I'm going after him."

Julio shook his head. "You heard him. I told you Gideon could take care of himself, but if he has to worry about watching after you, it may add to the danger." He held out his hand. "Step into my parlor, milady."

"But they're still shooting!" Serena wavered indecisively and then took Julio's hand and let him pull her out onto the scaffold. "If he's not here in two minutes, I'm going after him."

"Would you know what was so important that Gideon had to go back?" Julio asked.

"I have an excellent idea," Serena said with a sigh. "That lieutenant and the captain . . . I told Gideon it didn't matter, but I don't think I got through to him. What a time for his protective instincts to surface."

Julio's expression was suddenly as hard and relentless as Gideon's had been. "They hurt you? I didn't think there was any chance they'd be so stupid or I'd never have let you come here." He smiled and it was a sharklike baring of teeth. "Stay with her, Dane. I think I'll go and see if I can lend Gideon a hand."

"Not you too?" Serena wailed. "Has everyone here lost his sense of proportion?"

"You stay with Serena," Dane growled. "She's *my* sister, dammit. I should be the one who gets to go after them."

"Look, no one hurt me. The search was humiliating and degrading, but I wasn't hurt. It's over—"

"*Now* it's over." Gideon stood at the window, the gun shoved into the waistband of his jeans. He took Dane's hand and climbed out on the scaffold. "Let's get out of here. Mendino's men are a little confused with only a corporal to give the orders, but they're still fighting."

"What happened to the captain and the lieutenant?" Julio asked with a grin.

"They're . . . indisposed."

"A permanent condition?"

"I don't think so." Gideon's smile had a touch of the tiger. "But definitely a painful one."

"Can we please leave now?" Serena asked, shaking her head. "And you told me you didn't have a macho image of yourself."

"There wasn't anything macho about it." Gideon slipped an arm about her waist and grabbed onto a metal cord as Dane and Julio began to hoist the fragile scaffold up with the pulley ropes. Serena shivered as a gust of wind playfully shook the scaffold as if it were a toy. She carefully avoided looking down at the street. She had always hated those outside glass elevators and this was even worse, with not even a protective wall around them. "It was revenge. You would have done the same, if it had been me."

"No, I . . ." She stopped and then smiled reluctantly. "Well, maybe, but I would have chosen a more convenient time."

"I decided I might not get another chance. You might say the people of Castellano are a bit upset with the military. Those two might not have been around once the government fell."

The scaffold was now even with the roof, and Julio jumped onto the black tarred surface and then steadied the metal cord, which was fastened around the huge air-conditioning pump, as the other three left the scaffold.

"What now?" Gideon asked.

"We wait." Julio checked his watch. "But not for long, I hope."

"As long as we're not doing anything, why don't I run down and help Ross?" Dane asked. "All of this was kind of tame compared to the job you gave him."

"Tame?" Serena echoed blankly. "Blowguns, and scaffolds swinging hundreds of feet in the air? Tame?"

"Well, there's no real contact involved." Dane frowned discontentedly. "I was a little disappointed in you, Julio. I thought you'd provide more interesting entertainment."

"I'll try to do better in future," Julio said solemnly. He smothered a smile as he turned away and shaded his eyes. "You don't have to worry about Ross. His orders were to make a diversion and then get out. There wasn't much risk involved. Besides, I'm afraid you won't have time to join Ross at present." He pointed to a blue and white helicopter on the horizon. "There's our transport."

"Thank heavens," Serena murmured. All they needed was to lose Dane again.

The helicopter zoomed in, hovered, and then landed with pinpoint accuracy on the roof.

"Beautiful," Julio said admiringly. "I couldn't have done it better." He started for the helicopter. "You haven't lost your touch, Jeffrey." He opened the passenger door. "Wonderful landing, considering the wind up here."

"Wonderful landing, period," the pilot said flatly. "I thought I'd show you how it's done by the real pros, kid." His curly brown hair was torn by the wind as he stuck his head out the window. "Gideon, get them into the copter and let's move out."

Gideon, Serena, and Dane were already hurrying toward the helicopter. Julio had climbed into the seat beside the pilot, and the other three scrambled into the rear. Then the helicopter was lifting, turning, and speeding off over the rooftops of Mariba.

"Serena, Dane, this is Jeffrey Brenden," Julio said over his shoulder. "Jeffrey and I were partners in the air charter business, until he decided to retire." He grinned teasingly at the older man. "I decided he needed his red corpuscles revitalized, so I asked him to make the pickup. I didn't want the old man to get stale, vegetating on his coffee plantation."

"You asked me to make the pickup because I'm the best pilot in the Caribbean," Jeffrey corrected. "Even you would have had trouble with that wind."

"Maybe," Julio admitted. "Now let's see if you can do as good a job landing in the glade by Kate's tree house."

"A piece of cake, my boy." Jeffry smiled and turned the helicopter with faultless skill. "Just watch me."

It was almost over. Serena leaned back and closed her eyes. They were all safe, and soon it would be over. Her muscles suddenly felt as if they had dissolved into gelatin.

"All right?" Gideon's hand covered hers.

"Yes." She opened her eyes. "I guess I'm suffering from aftershock." She smiled shakily. "It's been quite a morning."

"Did you see that helicopter land?" Dane's gaze

was narrowed on Julio and Jeffrey quietly bantering in the cockpit and his tone was speculative. "Smooth as glass. I wonder how it feels to be able to do that."

Serena groaned inwardly. Knowing Dane, she was very much afraid he would soon be moved to find out.

She heard Gideon's amused chuckle, and felt his clasp tighten on her hand. "It could be worse," he whispered in her ear. "Jeffrey isn't exactly a sterling role model, but he's not a smuggler any longer."

"Smuggler?" Serena repeated faintly. "I don't know why I'm even surprised. You do have the most interesting friends."

He laughed again and settled back, as the helicopter took on added speed and left the environs of Mariba.

Eight

Jeffrey Brenden landed the helicopter in the glade in the rain forest with the consummate artistry of a butterfly settling on the petal of a fragile orchid. "There we go," he said with satisfaction. "Now could you do better, Julio?"

Julio shook his head. "No one could do better," he said with affection. He opened the door of the helicopter and stepped out onto the ground. "But don't get too cocky. We have a few more challenges to meet before you go home to Mariana."

"What challenges?" Serena asked warily. She had just been congratulating herself that the danger was almost past, and now Julio was speaking as if everything were only beginning. She jumped down beside him, closely followed by Gideon and Dane. "Haven't we had enough challenges for one day?"

Julio grinned. "Don't worry. You and Gideon and Dane are out of it from now on. Jeffrey is going to fly the three of you back to Santa Isabella in the Cessna. I'm taking the helicopter back to Mariba to join my men. Things are probably just beginning to liven up there about now." He glanced at his watch. "I have a rendezvous in forty-five minutes, so if you'll hop into the Cessna, Jeffrey will—"

"I'm going back with you," Dane interjected swiftly.

"No!" Serena's reaction was immediate and violent. "This is an uprising, not one of your parties, Dane. Do you think men as desperate as Mendino will be shooting blanks?"

"I'm going," Dane said stubbornly. "We left Ross back there, and it's only right I go back and help out."

"Very noble." Julio's gaze was shrewd as it searched Dane's face. "And besides, you didn't get in on the real action and you're jealous as hell."

Dane smiled. "Right."

Julio turned to Serena. "The only way you're going to keep him from going with me is to knock him out and hog-tie him." His smile was faintly regretful. "I should know. I went through the same kind of madness when I was a youngster. Only I didn't have to go looking for trouble. It always found me."

"But Dane's not like you," Serena protested.

Gideon took a step nearer and touched her arm. "Isn't he? Just look at them, Serena. They're cut from the same cloth."

Gideon was right, she realized gloomily. Gazing at them now was like looking at Siamese twins.

Dane and Julio's expressions, their attitudes, the way they perceived life as a glorious game, were exactly the same. Julio might be older and more experienced, but he had the same daredevil eccentricity she recognized as her brother's dominant trait.

"I'll take care of him," Julio promised. "And I'll bring him back to you in one piece."

"No one has to look out for me," Dane said with indignation. "Who knows? Maybe I'll be the one to have to take care of you."

"Maybe," Julio answered.

The two men exchanged smiles of perfect understanding.

Serena experienced a sudden twinge of sadness as if she'd lost something that would never be recovered. After all their years together, Dane wasn't going to need her very much longer. He would move on to other companions, and form other attachments as he grew older. It was entirely natural and right that this should be true, but the realization still brought with it a touch of melancholy. This adventure might be the last she would share with her brother.

Gideon's arm slid around her waist. "He'll be safe, love. You can trust Julio."

"I know." She also knew she had to let him go, cut the loving strings that had been as much for her own benefit as Dane's. She had never found it easy to let go of anyone she loved, and she loved Dane very much. She smiled with an effort. "Just promise me you'll stay off scaffolds."

Dane's smile illuminated his face. "That was an exception. I told you I don't do windows." He turned back toward the helicopter with barely leashed eagerness. "Come on, Julio, we'll be late for the rendezvous."

Julio's lips twitched. "Yes, *sir*."

Jeffrey Brenden came around the helicopter. "Be careful." He clapped Julio on the shoulder. "Luck doesn't last forever."

"I haven't noticed any signs of your luck fading away," Julio drawled.

"Because I had more than luck," Jeffrey said gruffly. "I had friends."

"And so do I." Julio's expression softened. "So do I, Jeffrey."

There was a silence more intimate than a handshake between them before Jeffrey turned jerkily away. "I'll go check out the Cessna. See you on Santa Isabella." He walked quickly toward the plane on the far side of the glade.

"You'll be back on Santa Isabella within the hour," Julio told Gideon. "And with any luck Dane and I will join you at the hotel for a midnight supper. Okay?"

"Okay," Gideon said with deliberate lightness. "I'll order a feast fit for Wellington's return from Waterloo. See that you're not late; I have a very temperamental chef."

"I'll instruct the junta it's essential they topple from power right on schedule. We wouldn't want to disrupt your plans." Julio turned toward Dane and jerked his thumb in the direction of the helicopter. "Hop into the passenger seat, Dane. Time's wasting."

"I know," Dane retorted caustically as he opened

the door. "I've been waiting for you to realize that. You're the one who's been holding up the works. I haven't heard so many touching farewells since I saw *The Wizard of Oz*. Take off your ruby slippers and let's get moving, Dorothy."

Julio's dark eyes were suddenly dancing. "Something tells me I may regret taking you with me. You don't have a fitting appreciation for the traditions. Heroic good-byes are *de rigueur* before engagements of this nature."

"Well, they seemed a little silly to me. It's not as if anything's going to happen to either of us."

"Ah, the immortality of youth." Julio shook his head with a sigh. "I can remember when I felt like that."

"Get into the helicopter," Dane said with a grin. "You're aging before my eyes and, if you get much more ancient, I don't know if I'm going to trust you to fly this thing. I hope you realize I don't appreciate your avuncular attitude. You're acting more like my father than—" He broke off, his expression sobering. "Oh damn, I forgot!" He turned away from the helicopter, his gaze on Serena. "With everything that's been happening, I forgot to tell you. Mendino contacted my father before Gideon arranged for the hostage switch."

Serena's breath stopped in her throat. "What?"

Dane's expression was troubled. "Lord, I'm sorry, Serena. I meant to tell you, but everything happened so fast. Mendino evidently thought he'd parlay his bets, so he hit my father with a ransom threat too. He told me my father was flying into Mariba this afternoon to discuss terms for my release."

Serena moistened her lips. "I see." She could feel Gideon's gaze on her face, but she didn't look at him. It wasn't over for her, either, then. Dane had his battle and she was going to have her own confrontation.

"I'll handle it," Dane said quickly. "You don't even have to see him. I'll just show him that his son and heir is no longer a prisoner and the Marlbrent line is in no immediately danger of being stomped into oblivion. That's all he wants to know anyway. You go on back to Santa Isabella."

She shook her head. "No, I'll do it." She turned to Julio. "Can you arrange for one of your men to pick him up at the airport and bring him here?" No, that wouldn't do, not here in the rain forest. She wanted to get Gideon away as quickly as possible. "That fishing village that you mentioned. Is there a place we can meet there?"

Julio nodded. "It shouldn't be a problem. This end of the island is practically uninhabited, and I have a friend who has a small cottage on the beach that should be safe." His lips curled. "Manuel won't be using it today. He's Consuela's brother, and you can bet he's going to want to be in on the kill in Mariba. Jeffrey can show you where the cottage is."

"Serena, I don't want you to—" Dane stopped. "Dammit, you swore you'd never see him again. I know what he did to you, and there's no reason why you should have to face him."

"I can deal with it.' Serena turned to Gideon. "You don't have to stay with me. I can meet you on Santa Isabella."

He slowly shook his head, his eyes narrowed on her face. "A bushwhacker?"

"The biggest bushwhacker of them all," she said softly. "And you can't help me with this one."

"What about your promise? We were going to share everything, remember?"

"I'll let you share and comfort." She smiled with an effort. "Later. I've got to face the bogeyman and convince myself that he never existed, or, if he did, that I created him."

"I'll have him delivered to Consuela's cottage." Julio turned away. "What's his name?"

"The Honorable Edwin Marlbrent." Serena's voice was laden with irony. "Or so *Burke's Peerage* refers to him. Personally, I don't agree with their opinion of my stepfather as 'honorable' in any way."

"We could arrange to have him brought to Santa Isabella," Gideon suggested.

"No. Santa Isabella is special for me. I don't want him to set foot there. Let it end where it began, here on Castellano." She glanced inquiringly at Julio. "If it won't endanger Gideon or Jeffrey?"

"In a few hours there won't be a *guardia* or a government," Julio said with a shrug. "And then no one will care less what you're doing here on Castellano."

"Well, that puts everything in perspective," Serena said wryly. "And it certainly deflates any idea I might have of my own importance in the scheme of things." She stepped back and waved. "Go on, don't let me keep you. We all have our own fish to fry." She smiled involuntarily at the accidental play on words. "And where could I choose a better spot to cook mine than your fishing village?"

Dane hesitated, and then climbed into the passenger seat, his expression still worried. "I'll see you tonight."

A few minutes later Gideon and Serena watched the helicopter lift off and then circle above the trees before turning toward Mariba.

The wind was warm and scented with salt as it brushed Serena's cheeks in a soft caress. She kicked off her high-heeled sandals and padded barefoot down to the surf. Her footprints in the wet sand immediately filled with water and then disappeared as if they had never been. Time was like that, she thought, it rushed in, covering, healing, and, if you were very lucky, taking away the scar entirely.

Gideon was watching her, his eyes intent, yet gentle. He sat down on an overturned rowboat drawn up out of reach of the tides. "He should be here soon."

"Yes." She gazed far down the deserted beach toward the tiny palmetto-thatched cottage. "I asked Jeffrey to send him as soon as he could." Her smile was bitter. "He won't like it. He prefers people to come to him."

He looked out over the horizon. "You hate him?"

"I did once. Now . . . I don't know. He's a terrible man, and I'll never understand how he can do the things he does, but he has some qualities I admire. He's brilliant, you know. He's one of the foremost financial advisers and bankers in England and, as far as I know, his business deals

are entirely honest. It's only in personal relationships that he's completely ruthless. What he can't
control, he has to destroy. He has to own the
people in his world." She turned and came back
to stand before him. "I cut the strings, but he
made me pay the price. I didn't know until I came
back to you how high that price had been. I
thought I'd shot my bushwhacker, but I hadn't,
I'd only run away from him."

She sat on the beach at his feet, her bare toes
digging in the sand. "I'd like to tell you all about
it." She smiled crookedly. "I know it's a little late.
Do you still want to hear it?"

"I want to hear it," he murmured. "I think it's
important I know."

"I think so too." She picked up a handful of
sand and let it sift slowly through her fingers.
"For one thing, it will illustrate how wrong you
were to think you had anything to learn from my
friends or family, any polish to acquire from them.
You're so far ahead they'd never catch up in a
hundred years." She paused. "I guess I should
start with my mother. There's no real harm in
her. She's just weak and selfish and can only see
as far as her checkbook. I think she may even
have loved my father; she always spoke of him as
if she did. He was a race car driver and after he
died . . ." She trailed off. "She likes money. She
needs money to complete herself. Edwin Marlbrent
had a great deal of money and he wanted an heir.
She married him and Dane was born eighteen
months later. He divorced her less than six months
after that." Her lips twisted. "Oh, don't make any
mistake about it. My mother was perfectly willing

to give him the divorce. It was a very amicable arrangement. My stepfather gave her a generous allowance for life, and she gave him custody of Dane. As she wasn't exactly the maternal type, the terms were exactly to her liking. A year later, she married someone else who suited her much better. Her French count had a lovely château in the wine country and no money so they dovetailed beautifully. The marriage suited my stepfather too. As long as she needed his money, he maintained full control over her and Dane." She paused. "And me."

"What were you doing while all this was going on?" Gideon asked. "Were you fond of Marlbrent while you were growing up?"

She shook her head. "He could be very charming, but he didn't waste it on me. I was away at school during their short marriage, and only saw them on those few holidays during that brief time." Her face softened. "But I was wild with joy when Dane was born. I'd always been a lonely child and I thought at last I'd have someone of my own to love. Of course, it didn't work out that way." Her face clouded. "No, I don't think my stepfather knew I existed as a human being." She paused. "Until he decided he could make use of me."

Gideon reached down and took her hand, holding it without speaking.

"I was seventeen and attending a convent school in Switzerland. I was very naive, incredibly so." She laughed mirthlessly. "You can't imagine how stupid I was. My stepfather appeared at the convent one day and whisked me away on a holiday to Italy. I was thrilled and happy and—I told you how charming he could be. I thought he actually *liked* me. I told myself that it was only children he had no use for, and now that I was almost grown up, he wanted to be my friend. He introduced me to Antonio del Montaldo in Florence, and Antonio traveled with us while we toured northern Italy. Antonio was handsome, charming, and a prince, and my stepfather heartily approved of him." She laughed again. "How could I resist? It was a damn fairy tale. We were married in Rome two weeks after my stepfather had taken me away from the convent. He even took his yacht out of dry dock and treated the newlyweds to a honeymoon trip to the Caribbean." Her lips curved in an ironic smile. "Just the three of us. I didn't think it unusual. I was floating—no, drowning—in charm. They were both being so wonderfully kind and affectionate and I gobbled it up like a hungry orphan. Antonio wasn't exactly passionate, but since I'd never had a lover, I didn't realize. . . . I was living in a dream world." She closed her eyes. "Until that night we docked at Mariba. I woke up and Antonio wasn't in the cabin. I got out of bed and went looking for him." She stopped and was silent a moment. "I found him. He was in my stepfather's bed. My stepfather was making love to him." She could feel Gideon's hand tighten on her own, but she didn't open her eyes. "I was stunned and almost hysterical. I can remember screaming at them, and the two of them looking at me as if I were a mosquito that had caused them a minor annoyance." She ran her tongue over her lips to moisten them. "Then my stepfather sat up in bed and began to speak to me. His voice was very cold and reasonable. He was in love with Antonio, and in his position any rumor of homosexuality was out of the question. It would have seriously compromised his social and business status in London. There had already been a few suspicions voiced regarding his lack of female companionship since the divorce from my mother. The sensible thing to do was to bring Antonio into the family." Her lips curled bitterly. "That's the very word he used. Sensible. Our marriage tie would throw a cloak of respectability on his association with Antonio. Now all I had to do was to be a good little girl and keep my mouth shut while they used me." Her eyes opened to reveal eyes glittering with remembered pain. "I think that's what threw me into a tailspin. Neither one of them had ever cared about me. They were only *using* me. I guess I went a little crazy. I ran out of the cabin, and down the gangplank. I didn't know where I was running, or—"

"You were running to me." Gideon's voice was velvet with tenderness. "It was the time for us to come together."

She met his eyes. "I believe that now, but that night I was confused and upset. I had suffered a shock that had shaken me to the foundations and sent me in a daze wandering through Mariba. I don't even know how I got into that bar where you found me. Oh, I was brimful of a convent idea of sin. I'd taken a marriage vow and, even if I'd been duped, I couldn't reconcile myself to the idea of breaking that vow." She shook her head in wonder as she looked back on that bewildered child. "Perhaps my stepfather even relied on that convent training. It wouldn't surprise me."

"You shouldn't have left me. We could have worked everything out if we'd been together."

"He would have destroyed you," she said simply. "I didn't dare even mention you. I told you, what he couldn't control, he destroyed. He was a very powerful man and you were just getting started. That night I lay awake and tried to think of a way out, but I knew there was only one solution. I had to let them use me, until I could gather the strength to break free." She determinedly blinked back the tears. "That first year was bad. I wanted to run back to you a hundred times a day."

"But you didn't."

"No, I started to close you out instead." She lifted his palm and cradled it against her cheek. "Remember when I told you that everything I love becomes an obsession with me? When I came to you, I was starved for affection and you gave me everything I'd ever dreamed about. I had been alone and suddenly you held out the promise that I'd never be alone again. I loved you so *much* it nearly killed me. The only way I could survive was to shut you out entirely. If I couldn't have all of you, I didn't want memories. I painted the mental picture I wanted to see and put you in the past where you couldn't hurt me."

"You managed very well." Gideon's voice held a thread of pain.

She shook her head. "I thought I had, but it all fell apart when I saw you. Though I still had a king-size hang-up from repressing what I felt for you all those years. I think that was why I had trouble making a commitment." Her lips lovingly brushed his palm. "I finished my education and then made a deal with my stepfather. I would stay married to Antonio on two conditions—that I didn't have to live with them and that he would give me custody of Dane."

"He went along with it?"

"He loved Antonio. I think perhaps Antonio was the only person he ever really did love." Her lips curled. "And Dane was no personal loss to him. He'd been shipped away to schools since he was practically an infant. My stepfather probably thought I'd come crawling back to him when I found myself facing the world without a dime in my pocket."

"But you didn't go back to him?"

"No, but you were right, I gave up a few things. My work . . . and you." She kissed his palm again. "But you wouldn't stay in the nice little slot in my past where I had put you. You're a very obstinate man, Gideon Brandt, and I'll thank God for it every day for the rest of my life." She raised her eyes and finished gravely. "I love you and you'd better get accustomed to the idea that I'll never give up this particular obsession until the day I die."

"I can hardly wait." The long crescent lines in his cheeks deepened as he smiled down at her. "I've never been anyone's obsession before. I expect to enjoy the hell out of it." His smile faded. "I wish you'd let me stay. I don't want you to have to face that bastard alone."

She shook her head. "I can't say I'm looking forward to it, but I have to do it on my own. He dominated my life for a long time and, even when I got away from him, he still loomed larger than life. Don't you see, I ran away from him. I've been avoiding him for nine years, because I was afraid to face him again." Her expression was desperately in earnest as she tried to make him understand. "I thought I had beaten him when I took Dane and left him, but you can't really claim victory until you come to terms with what you fear. I have to prove he's not important to me anymore. It's the only way I'm ever going to be able to shoot this bushwhacker out of the saddle." She drew a deep breath. "Do you understand?"

He became very still. "Yes, I understand," he said slowly. "And I think you may be right." His gaze lifted from her face to the thatched cottage down the beach. "Is that your bushwhacker coming toward us?"

She followed his gaze and went tense. She hurriedly rose to her feet and nervously brushed the sand from her skirt. Edwin Marlbrent was still far down the beach, but she could feel the familiar fear and tension gripping her.

Gideon stood up and his hand clasped her shoulder in encouragement. "Good shooting, partner." He started down the beach toward the cottage. "I'll see you later."

She scarcely heard him. Her attention was focused on her stepfather coming toward her. In his late fifties, he was an attractive and imposing man. His dark hair was slightly flecked with gray and his tall, heavily muscular body was clad with faultless elegance in an expensive dark business suit. He was frowning as his highly glossed shoes sank into the sand with every step. He had always abhorred the fact that the natural elements of nature were beyond his control and generally avoided exposing himself to the minor defeat they represented.

Serena automatically ran her hand through her rumpled hair to tidy it. She tried desperately to relax, but the habit of years was strong, and she felt as if she were encased in an iron straitjacket.

Gideon had come abreast of Marlbrent and he stopped, his head tilted to the side as he leisurely studied the older man. Marlbrent stopped, too, his frown deepening in puzzlement.

Gideon's lean, whipcord body was dressed, as usual, in jeans and boots. The sleeves of his forest green shirt were rolled to the elbow revealing his tanned forearms, and his sunstreaked hair was ruffled by the breeze. In his elegantly sophisticated apparel and with his imposing, heavily built physique, Marlbrent should have made Gideon seem to dwindle in comparison. Yet this wasn't the case. Gideon's strength dominated the scene with absolutely no effort on his part.

Gideon suddenly cast a glance at Serena over his shoulder, his eyes gleaming with humor and a touch of mischief. Then he turned back to Marlbrent, extended his index finger as if he were aiming a gun, and slowly made the motion of pulling the trigger.

Serena's laughter rang out over the deserted beach as she saw her stepfather's expression of befuddlement and outrage. Abruptly her tension and the ingrained fear of years disappeared as if it had never existed.

Without another glance, or speaking a single word, Gideon passed Marlbrent and continued down the beach toward the cottage. His stride was a careless saunter, but his bearing was totally indomitable.

Nine

It was done.

Serena watched her stepfather walk away and then turned once again to face the soothing rush of the waves against the shore. The episode hadn't been pleasant, but now it was over she was experiencing a singing exuberance and a profound sense of freedom. She would give Marlbrent a few minutes to leave the village, and then she would find Gideon. There was no hurry, and she needed a little time to absorb exactly what had happened here today.

It was over fifteen minutes later that she picked up her shoes and strolled slowly back to the cottage.

Jeffrey Brenden's keen brown eyes searched her face. "Are you all right?" he asked gruffly. "Gideon asked me to keep an eye on that big guy, but you didn't seem to be in any trouble."

She smiled. "No trouble at all. Where's Gideon?"

"Gone."

She became still. "Gone?"

"He said he'd be back in a couple of hours." He looked at his watch. "We talked for a bit before he set out, but I guess he left about fifteen minutes after Marlbrent arrived, so he shouldn't be long now."

"But where did he go?"

"The rain forest. He had me give him directions to the tree house."

The rain forest. A ripple of shock went through her, followed by an instant and sweeping rejection. What could have possessed him to go back there, after what he had gone through last night? She felt panic clutch at her as she thought of Gideon alone and reliving that nightmare by himself. "No," she whispered. "It doesn't make any sense. Why?" Her gaze lifted to Jeffrey's face. "I have to go after him. Will you show me the way?"

"Sure, if you think it's better to follow him." He raised a brow as he glanced down at the high-heeled sandals in her hand. "Those aren't very practical trekking shoes."

"They're all I have with me. I left my jeans and tennis shoes at the tree house when Julio brought me this outfit. He thought that purse with the bamboo handles wouldn't be carried by a woman wearing jeans."

"Sounds like Julio." There was a touch of pride in Jeffrey's voice. "He pays attention to details." He turned away. "I might be able to find you a pair of Manuel's sandals in the cottage. They'll be too big, but at least you won't be turning your ankle."

"Hurry. Please hurry."

Jeffrey looked back over his shoulder. "Don't worry. I'll see that you're with Gideon in forty-five minutes, tops."

It was closer to thirty minutes when Kate's tree came into view. It was strange, but since Julio had told her the story of Kate and Beau Lantry that night while they were waiting for Gideon to return from Mariba, Serena now always thought of the tree house as belonging to Kate rather than Julio.

"Here you are," Jeffrey said. "Gideon must still be up there since we didn't run into him on the way over here." He stopped under the tree, his eyes twinkling. "I think I'll go back to the cottage and wait for you there. I don't believe either of you will need me anymore."

"Thank you, Jeffrey." She began to climb the rungs of the ladder. "I appreciate you bringing—" She broke off as she looked over her shoulder and realized Jeffrey had gone. She tilted back her head and called, "Gideon, Are you there? Is everything all right?"

"I'm here."

Serena felt relief pour through her. As far as she could tell from his voice, he couldn't be suffering any traumatic upset. "I'll be right up. I was worried when you ran off like that. If you wanted to come back here, why the devil didn't you wait for me?" She stepped onto the platform. The door was wide open as it had been last night and she could see Gideon sitting on the mattress at the far end of the room. "I didn't spend that much time with my honorable stepfather."

"How did it go?"

"Well. Wonderfully well. I feel . . . free. It wasn't

easy, but—" Her eyes widened in surprise as she gazed around the tiny room.

The entire house was brimming, exploding with flowers. Brilliant coral and cream-colored wild orchids had been thrust into the formerly empty black vase on the nightstand and into the rattan holders on the walls until they were overflowing with fragrance and beauty. The tall vase in the corner now held maidenfern and exotic white and gold blossoms. Wild flowers had even been strewn over the denim cover of the mattress next to the window.

"Do you like it?" Gideon asked quietly.

"It's beautiful." Serena's gaze returned to his face. "*You've* been out in the rain forest picking flowers?"

He nodded. "Jeffrey told me a little about Kate, and how she had loved this little tree house and everything about the rain forest. How she always filled her world with flowers and tried to make the best of life. It reminded me of some of the things you said to me on the beach."

She crossed the room and dropped to her knees on the mattress beside him. "What things? I remember rambling on about any number of subjects."

"About coming to terms with the past." His gaze met her own with grave tranquillity. "I realized I'd been so busy running away from the memory of Na Peng that I was letting it poison my judgment of the present. So I walked back through the rain forest and tried to see what Kate had seen here. The flowers and the birds, the sounds and . . . the beauty."

"Did it work?"

"Not at first. My stomach was tied in knots; I felt sick. I wanted you beside me, holding my hand."

She reached out and gathered both of his hands, threading her fingers through his in a silent bonding. "I'll hold your hands now. I'll hold them forever."

"Forever. You finally got around to saying it."

She smiled shakily. "I'm a little slow, but I always manage to get there eventually."

"So do I." Gideon's smile was warm and tender, lighting up the room, lighting up the world. "After a while I found it got better and, by the time I got to the tree house, I was seeing Kate's world as she had seen it. The ugliness was gone, lost somewhere in the past. It's possible that it may not stay lost and I may need a little help to push it back when—"

"When it tries to ambush you?" Serena finished softly. "Once upon a time a very wise man told me that whenever the ugliness comes back, all we have to do is think of something beautiful and it will fade away again."

He chuckled. "I'm wonderful at solving other people's problems. But I'm lucky, I don't have to *think* of something beautiful. I have it right in front of me." He bent his head and kissed her with lingering sweetness. "Say you love me again. I like to hear it."

"I love you," she whispered. "I'll always love you and stand beside you. I'll give you my strengths and my weaknesses, my mind and my heart. There won't be a day or a month or a year I won't need and want you and not a second when you won't fill my life. Is that enough for you?"

He smiled with a joy as radiant as the emotion reflected on her face. "No, but it will do for a start. You've got the next seventy years or so to get it right.'

She laughed. She felt wild and free and positively dizzy with happiness. "You're a hard man to please."

"Not at the moment." He pulled her into his arms. "I couldn't be more pleased at the moment."

"Are we going back to the cottage?" She snuggled closer into his arms. "Jeffrey said he'd wait for us there. I guess we should be thinking about starting for Santa Isabella and beginning to make plans."

"Soon." His warm lips brushed her temple and his hand began to stroke the dark silk of her hair. "Now I think we'll sit here for a while and smell the flowers and listen to the birds and just be together. We can think about the future tomorrow. Right now, the present seems mighty sweet to me."

Serena closed her eyes in sublime contentment and relaxed against his lean, hard strength. All the dark yesterdays had faded into oblivion and all the bright tomorrows were yet to come. They could rest and enjoy what they had won.

For a long, long time, they sat in the tree house, surrounded by flowers, the song of the birds, and the magical reality of their love. And she discovered that Gideon was right. The present was more than sweet enough.

THE EDITOR'S CORNER

This summer is going to be one of the best ever! That's not a weather forecast, but a reading report. There will be some very special publishing events you can look forward to that reach just beyond the regular LOVESWEPT fare—which, of course, is as wonderful as always. Alas, I'm limited by space, so I have to try to restrain my urge to describe these books in loving detail. (How I regret that brevity is not one of my virtues!)

During the first week of next month, a brilliant and heartwarming love story will appear in your bookstores—**NEVER LEAVE ME** by Margaret Pemberton. (This Bantam book may be housed in romance sections of some stores, general fiction of others. Do look for it or ask your bookseller to pull a copy for you. Trust me, this is a story you will *not* want to miss!) British, a mother of five, and a wonderfully stylish and talented storyteller, Margaret was first published by us in December 1985. That novel, **GODDESS,** was the compelling love story of Valentina, a mysterious young woman who became a legendary film star, and Vidal, the passionate, powerful, unattainable man who was her discoverer and director. This story often comes hauntingly to my mind. Now, in **NEVER LEAVE ME**, Margaret tells the equally haunting, yet quite different story of Lisette de Valmy, of her forbidden love and a secret that very nearly shatters her happiness. The man she will marry, Greg Derring, is nothing short of marvelous . . . and the climax of the book is so full of emotional richness and poignancy that I dare you to finish the story dry-eyed.

The following month you have an enormous, happy surprise—the zany, chilling, sexy **HOT ICE** by Nora Roberts. I bet you've loved Nora's more than forty romances during the last few years as much as I have. (Yes, we do love books published by our honorable competitors!) How were we so lucky that we got to publish a Nora Roberts book? Well, because what she is writing for us is outside the range of her Silhouette love stories. **HOT ICE** is a romantic suspense, a zesty adventure tale with a grand love story between an ice cream heiress, Whitney, and a criminal—a real, non-garden variety thief with plenty of street smarts—Doug. They're the sassiest, most delightful couple I've encountered since *Romancing The Stone* and the first episode

(continued)

of *Moonlighting*! In the back of **HOT ICE** you'll get an excerpt of Nora's next romantic suspense novel, **SACRED SINS,** an absolutely breathtaking tale, which will be published in December, on sale the first week of November.

THE DELANEY DYNASTY LIVES ON! In July we will distribute a free sampler to tease you unmercifully about the marvelous trilogy **THE DELANEYS OF KILLAROO,** which gives you the love stories of three dynamite ladies of the Australian branch of the Delaney family. But we won't torment you long, because the full works go on sale in early August. Of course these fabulous books were written by the ladies of **THE SHAMROCK TRINITY:** Kay Hooper, Iris Johansen, and Fayrene Preston.

I must rush along now so that, hopefully, I can tantalize you with a few words on the LOVESWEPTs for next month.

NOT A MARRYING MAN by Barbara Boswell, LOVE-SWEPT #194, reintroduces you to a shameless rogue you met briefly before, Sterne Lipton. (Remember him? He's the brother of the heroine of **LANDSLIDE VICTORY.**) Well, Sterne has more than met his match in Brynn Cassidy. When she finds out he's wagered a bundle on getting her into bed, she sets out to teach the ruthless bachelor a ruthless lesson. But soon both of them are wildly, madly, completely in love with one another . . . and in deep hot water. Funny, touching, **NOT A MARRYING MAN** is one more superb love story from Barbara, whose work never fails to delight.

I can't tell you what a pleasure it was for me to work on Sara Orwig's witty and wonderful, **WIND WARNING,** LOVE-SWEPT #195. Savannah Carson and Mike Smith crash into one another on boats in Lake Superior. Mike quite literally falls overboard for the lovely lady, too, but grave danger denies them the freedom to stay together. **WIND WARNING** should carry a cautionary label—its heroine and hero just might steal your heart.

Never, ever has a tent in the wilderness held a more exciting couple than in Hertha Schulze's **SOLID GOLD PROSPECT,** LOVESWEPT #196. Heroine Nita Holiday is a woman with whom each of us can readily identify as we learned so well in Hertha's first LOVESWEPT, **BEFORE AND AFTER,** because she's an avid romance reader. Mr. Right seems to her to have stepped right off the page of a LOVESWEPT when she sets eyes on Matt Lamartine. And

(continued)

Matt can scarcely tear himself away from the beguiling woman whose background is so different from his own that it shakes him right down to his toes. From New York to Chicago to the vast, romantic wilderness of Canada, Nita and Matt pursue passion . . . and the understanding that can make their love last forever. An utterly sensational romance.

As the New Year began some months ago I was thinking back over the years, remembering the writers with whom I've had long relationships. Among them, of course, is Sandra Brown whose warm friendship I have enjoyed as much as her superb professionalism. One of the many things I admire about Sandra is that she never rests on her laurels. She constantly challenges herself to achieve new writing goals— and all of us are the beneficiaries. In her next romance, **DEMON RUMM,** LOVESWEPT #197, you'll see another instance of how Sandra continues to expand her mastery of her craft for she writes this story exclusively from the hero's point-of-view. Rylan North is a famous, enigmatic, perfectionistic movie idol. Tapped to star as Demon Rumm, the late husband of the heroine, Kirsten, he moves into her house . . . her life . . . her very soul. Sultry and sensitive, this romance is one of Sandra's most memorable. A true keeper.

We hope you will be as excited as we are over the line-up of LOVESWEPTs and other novels that we've developed for a sensational summer of reading.

With every good wish,

Carolyn Nichols

Carolyn Nichols
 Editor
LOVESWEPT
Bantam Books, Inc.
666 Fifth Avenue
New York, NY 10103